Santa 2020

the Final Ride

Also by Jane Shoup

Down in the Valley
Spirit of the Valley
Will of the Valley
Knightfall
The Restoration
Zan, Birth of a Legend
The Key
A Choice of Captors
Ammey McKeaf, Book One: The Chronicles of Azulland
Heirs to the Throne, Book Two: The Chronicles of Azulland
Into Shadow, Book Three: The Chronicles of Azulland
Charity Cases
The Time Tunnel of August Kaplan

Copyright © 2021 by Jane Shoup
ISBN: 9781735164854

Dedicated to all of you on the Nice list and to roughly one third of you on the Naughty list.

You know who you are.

Glossary:

CAE: Chief Administrative Elf

HHE: Human-height elf

TGB: The Great Beyond

HCE: Human current events

HCEU: Human current events update

Elfkin: Young elf, typically under the age of six

STT: Santa's think tank

PSI: Preliminary Santa Interview

DCV: Direct Contact Visit

Nipst: North Pole Sky Tram

RDHQ: Reindeer delegate headquarters

SKI: Santa knowledge implant

Glide disc: Conveyance that first lifts passenger or item centimeters off the ground.

BOOK I: THE CHOICE

Chapter One
The Showdown

The hard soles of Marencourt's red-satin shoes announced his approach as he made his way across the marble floor to the great man's office. Most manor elves wore soundless satin slippers but not him. He had earned the right to make a bit of noise when he chose. As he approached the twelve-foot wooden doors, (which, to an outsider, might have looked rather enormous to a standard-height elf such as himself who did not even reach the fancy brass doorknobs) he gestured once as if conducting a great orchestra and the doors flung open. It was overkill, but it was the principal of the thing.

Marencourt clasped his hands behind his back as he went toward the grumpy old man slumped in the wide leather desk chair turned so that he could stare out the window with what had become his usual long face. What the man should have been doing was facing the desk and the piles of letters thereon. He should have been reading, thinking and making plans. The problem, and it was a big problem, perhaps even a crisis, was that Santa was no longer fulfilling his obligations which were clearly stipulated in the contract.

Marencourt was stuck with him for another four weeks and three days, so, clearly, it was time to play hardball. Having rounded the desk, Marencourt stopped short with a scowl on his face. "What number are you on?"

Santa's gaze shifted to him. "What?" he asked irritably.

Santa had heard him perfectly well so Marencourt merely lifted one bushy brow in impatience.

"Oh, I don't know," Santa hedged. "Must be thirty." He sniffed lightly. "Forty."

"It is *thirteen*," Marencourt corrected heatedly.

Santa looked back out the window with a sneer. "Why ask the question when you know the answer?"

Marencourt's inclination was to rage at him, but his four hundred and six years of experience in the job told him he needed to rein in his infamous temper and concentrate on the task at hand. All of elfdom was in order, but the fat lump before him was mucking the works up. The simple truth was that the job could not get done without Santa and the clock was ticking. The situation could not be allowed to continue.

The CAE (chief administrative elf) turned and walked, crossing the thick braided rug that covered the wide-planked wood floor. He noticed curious maids peeking into the office from what they thought were discreet alcoves in the hallway, and he glared at them before slamming the doors shut with a flick of his hands.

He resumed his pacing until he stopped in front of the floor-to-ceiling bookshelves containing leather bound tomes of each Santa's history, including their naughty-nice lists. The volumes were arranged by eras, each represented by a different Santa and different colored leather. The CAE frowned thoughtfully. He realized it had been an exceedingly difficult year for Santa. The poor man had lost his wife, his beloved Sera, and the loss had shattered him. As if that weren't enough to contend with, there was a pandemic. Covid-19 was not the earth's first pandemic, but it was the first for most people living. Many had experienced hardship because of it. Some had suffered death, heartbreak and tragedy.

The elf rounded the desk again. "Grief still clouds your mind and heart," he began in a more temperate tone. "We all loved Mrs. Claus, too." Santa's frown darkened. He was probably insulted to have his loss compared with theirs. So be it then. Enough Mister Nice Elf. "But you have duties and there can be no more delay in attending them," he added sternly.

Santa turned in the swivel chair and then stood with a formidable expression.

Pah! Did the old man seriously believe he could outglare him? Marencourt crossed his arms and craned his neck to connect eye to eye. "Read the letters and make arrangements!"

Santa crossed his arms stubbornly. "And if I don't?"

"I hoped you would not say that," Marencourt replied coolly. A flicker of confusion crossed Santa's face. Had the man actually forgotten? "The agreement, Santa," the elf said meaningfully. "The contract. The pact. Age old and iron clad." Santa's confusion seemed to escalate. "If you need to be reminded, reread it." The confusion on Santa's face slowly morphed to one of concern. Good! He needed to be concerned with the calendar winding down and so much left to do.

Santa uncrossed his arms and faced the room with slumping shoulders. "What if I don't have it in me?"

"You do," Marencourt stated emphatically. "You would not have been chosen if you did not." He paused and then said, "There are four weeks and three days left and you must fulfill your duties." Santa whirled back to face him and his resentment was evident again. However, enough had been said and so Marencourt started for the door. "Paragraph one hundred and one," he said enunciating precisely. "Subsection B." He waved a hand and a door opened before he reached it. He walked through and it closed behind him.

Chapter Two
Paragraph 101, Subsection B

S anta sat heavily. He leaned forward and drummed his fingers on the desk searching his memory for what Marencourt had been talking about. Paragraph one hundred and one? What was the topic of paragraph one hundred and one? Obviously, it was of vital importance, the proverbial ace up Marencourt's elaborate puffed sleeve.

Fine. He would read it again. He had not laid eyes on the contract since before his term began. Naturally, he and Sera had been apprised of what the Claus's roles entailed and had happily agreed. What a thrill it had been, not to mention the honor of their lives. They had been selected from thousands of other qualified candidates, and it had been the perfect existence for them. They had not hesitated to accept and they had never once regretted it. He smiled thinking about it, but his pleasant expression quickly faded and he heaved a sigh.

In the spring, Sera had grown ill and died. That was not supposed to have happened. They were supposed to have experienced the full term together and taken the final ride together. The reign of each Claus was for fifty-eight years beginning and ending on the second Sunday of January. Over the centuries, the elves had arrived at that specific number to achieve maximum efficiency from each Claus. The job was not as easy as most people thought. It came with tremendous responsibility.

Twice before Sera, a Mrs. Claus had passed away before the end of her husband's term. He and Sera had been told as much, but assumed it would not happen to them. No one had ever been as happily and completely joined as they were. Santa rose from his chair. His right knee ached and so he limped over to select the volume on the bookshelf that contained their story. He went to the curved sofa in front of the hearth and sat. How often he and Sera had sat here together watching the dance of flames around and through the kindling

"Nog, please," he said. "Extra rum."

Steeling himself, he cracked open the book and marveled at the photograph of Sera and himself in their engagement photo. He was thirty years of age; she was thirty-two and so lovely. Sera. How he loved her. God in heaven, how he missed her. Below the photograph was the caption *Westcott/Claus. January 13, 1963- January 10, 2021.*

A four-foot panel in the wall that concealed a servant's passageway slid open and Cassarina came in with a tray of nibbles and a tall glass of egg nog sprinkled with nutmeg, the way he liked it. She set the tray on a floating surface that had followed her.

"Thank you, Ree."

"I am always pleased to serve you, Santa. Do you need anything else?"

"No. I probably don't need this either." He patted his bulging tummy.

She gave him a gentle smile and her gaze flicked down the page of the book on his lap. Sadness troubled her face. "I miss her."

"So do I. Every waking moment."

Cassarina turned and left. She was a sweet elf who had been devoted to Sera.

Santa took a sip of the creamy drink before setting the glass back down. He turned the page and skimmed the paragraph that detailed his information. His birth name, Bart James Westcott, was written above a fat-cheeked baby picture. Below it was the rest of his biographical data. His birthdate, July 9, 1933, the names of his parents, his stepfather, his younger half-sibling, Martha, his grandparents. In fact, his full lineage was detailed.

The state of his general health was notated along with a list of illnesses and injuries. Any life experiences with significant impact were recorded including that he'd lost his father in the Second World War.

In summation: (the report read) 'He is a bright, curious boy who frequently fails to achieve his full potential.'

Politeness – 6.25
Kindness – 8.75
Punctuality – 3
Attention span – 4
Courage – 9
The list of traits and behaviors went on.
Patience – 5
Concentration – 6.5
Social skills – 8
Problem solving- 9
Manners – 4.9

When all categories were tallied, the grand total added up to 512. He had been assessed at three different ages, when he was ten, twenty-three and thirty and the marks remained oddly consistent.

He glanced over photographs of himself at different stages of his life. He'd been a fairly good student and played baseball with school teams. As a young man, he had gone to the state university and studied packaging engineering. After graduation, he'd volunteered and served in the army during the Vietnam War. As the son of a veteran who'd paid the ultimate price in defense of his country, he'd felt compelled to go, but he had loathed it from day one.

Eleven months into his tour, his right leg had been badly damaged in combat. He'd been airlifted out, his leg mended as much as possible. Secretly, he'd wondered if the injury had ultimately saved his life since it resulted in a medical discharge. Back in civilian life, he got a job with a box manufacturer as a floor manager. It had not been an exciting job, but it was good enough.

One nasty morning in November of 1960, he went into a doughnut shop on his way to work and saw the lady who would change his life. She was facing forward, waiting for her order. She had dark, softly curling hair, the sides swept back and held with a pink barrette. She wore a belted burgundy-plaid coat and brown boots. The neck of a bright pink turtleneck sweater was all that showed of her clothing underneath her coat.

As if drawn by his staring, although he was trying to be discreet about it, she looked at him and smiled shyly before facing forward again. A blush crept into her pretty face. Oh, what that blush did to his heart.

The memory of the instant she first looked at him was etched in his mind, a permanent snapshot. It was one of many, but it was special because it was the first.

Fortunately, she had a large order, having gotten enough doughnuts for her workmates plus a paper cup of coffee for herself. As she pulled out the handles on the side of the cup, he stepped over to offer assistance carrying it to her car and she accepted. In the few minutes it took for her to prepare her coffee the way she liked, with cream and sugar, and to get her loaded up and on her way, he had given his name and learned hers. She was a teacher and it was a teacher workday. She said that she rarely stopped at that doughnut shop. *Fate*, whispered in his brain. He believed it to this day.

He asked for permission to call and she gave her telephone number, perhaps hurried by a stinging sleet that he barely noticed. As she left, he felt as if he'd been touched by an angel. It therefore came as no surprise that she had been named after a highly ranked angel.

He flipped the page and came to the report on Sera. Birth name: Seraphina Elizabeth Wells. She outscored him in all categories which had never been a surprise to him. Sera, who particularly enjoyed teaching the third grade, loved children. So did he. They were heartbroken to discover they were unable to have their own. It was one of many reasons the Claus mission had been so perfect for them. And it had been a mission, a life choice and a magnificent gift, all rolled into one.

'Term, January 13, 1963-January 10, 2021.' Santa tapped the date with his finger. He had agreed to it. They both had. But then she'd grown ill. She had died in their bed with him at her side. He had not yet fully accepted it when, moments later, her body had begun to sparkle and glow. The light had grown blinding and, in a blink, she was gone. Vanished. Gone to the other place, The Great Beyond.

Santa's breath caught from the shock of a sudden realization. The other place. The fourth level of heaven. That was what Marencourt had been talking about. That was what paragraph one hundred and one, subsection B was about. "I need a copy of paragraph one hundred and one of the contract," he uttered.

He set down the book, rose and began to pace. He kept in motion until Vestor, a human-height elf, hurried in with a rolled piece of parchment, bowed and then passed it over. "Here you are, Your Majesty. Page twenty-six with paragraph one hundred and one in its entirety."

Santa scanned the paragraph. It was just as he feared. "I should have been reminded of this."

"I beg your pardon?"

Santa saw that Vestor looked stricken. "I didn't mean you, Vestor. Thank you for bringing it so promptly."

The tall elf bowed again before leaving.

Santa returned to his desk, donned his reading spectacles and read the page word for word. The gist of the aforementioned paragraph was that he and Sera were entitled to the fourth level of Heaven after the conclusion of a successful term. Most people good enough for TGB, The Great Beyond, went to either the first or second level. Even the saintliest humans were only granted access to the third level, but Sera was waiting for him in the fourth level.

The contract was clear. They were eligible for the TGB Level 4 following the conclusion of a *successful* term. Failure of this, (this was subsection B) would result in the less than satisfactory party being deposited where they would have had they had lived out their human existence. For him, that meant level one, at best. "Marencourt," he bellowed.

The door opened and Marencourt stood there. "Did you call?" he asked calmly.

Santa seethed at the elf's insolence, but he was determined not to show it. He looked at him over the rim of the spectacles which had slid down his nose. "You should have reminded me."

Marencourt gave a slight shrug. "I am aware of the stipulations of all contracts I have signed," he replied archly. "I assumed you were, as well."

Santa squinted. "I will read the letters," he stated.

Marencourt gave a single nod. "And not all from the easy pile."

"I am aware of that."

"Christmas is in eighteen days. You have a lot of work to do. There are the letters to be read and arrangements to be made for each case. And the selection committee for your replacement is ready to reconvene. The final nominees have been decided and the choice must be made forthwith. Your input is mandated."

"Name the day and time and I will be there."

"And you need a haircut." The CAE turned to go, highly pleased with himself.

"Marencourt."

Marencourt turned back to face him.

"Had I failed," Santa said. "What would have happened to Sera?"

Marencourt drew back as if offended. "Mrs. Claus would not have been penalized. She could have visited you … wherever you went. That's the privilege of level four. Sera Claus was exceptional."

"While you see me as a failure?"

Marencourt took a moment to reply. "On the contrary," he replied earnestly. "You have been excellent until these last months. You were worthy. Be worthy again. You only have four weeks and three days left in your term, but the world is enduring a difficult year. People need you. Children need you."

Santa sighed tiredly. "What a year to be Santa."

Marencourt sniffed. "There have been worse."

"Have there?" Santa snapped with annoyance.

Marencourt's eyes narrowed. "I have assisted seven administrations and seen years of starvation and disease. Depressions, genocide, wars. So, yes, there have been worse." He paused. "Having said that, on the whole, this past year on earth has been bleak," he relented. "Which is why Christmas is so needed. Miracles are needed. You are needed." Having concluded, Marencourt bowed his head and shut the door.

Santa felt chastened as he reached for a letter.

Chapter Three
The Letters

Santa lay on his stomach atop a massage table as he read his fifty-sixth letter of the year through the hole in the headrest as Borivir, an HHE (human-height elf) vigorously massaged his back. Between Santa's body being jostled, not having his reading glasses on and deciphering the writing of a child, it was not the easiest task. So far, he'd read,

Dear Santa,
This is Liam Alan Easton. I am six. I will be seven in January. I live in the apartments behind Johnson Elementary school in Dayton. 218-C Johnson Street is my address. Can I change my mind about what I asked you to get me? I wanted a remote-control car like Derek has, but I won't get that if my brother can get good essay-tees.

Santa stuck the letter out to the side. "What does this say?" he asked in a muffled voice. "Asaytease? A Mercedes? What?"

Borivir glanced in the direction of the letter as he put more coconut oil in his hands and rubbed them together to warm them. "He'll give up the toy he wanted," he replied, "a remote-control car, if his brother can get a good score on his SATs." Bori clucked his tongue. "Such a sweet boy. The kid he mentioned, Derek, is a tyrant. The remote-control vehicle did *not* come from us."

SATs. How was he supposed to pull that off? Santa let the letter fall to the floor and tried to relax and enjoy the massage. Bori was the best massage therapist in the city.

"Shall I finish reading the letter?" Bori asked as he began a chopping motion on Santa's back.

"Sure," Santa grunted out.

"'My brother's name is Tommy Leonard. He has a different last name than me. He is a really good brother. Sincerely, Liam.'"

"You can't buy a test score," Santa said in a vibrating voice.

"Although didn't a few people try this year?" Bori jested. He thoroughly enjoyed keeping up with human current events.

Santa couldn't reply intelligently, because he did not keep up with current events. He hadn't since the mid-seventies. Obviously, Liam's story needed more looking into and so did a few others that had intrigued him. He would go to the viewing room after his massage and see what there was to see.

A half hour later, Santa headed to the viewing room wearing his favorite fleece pants and an open, unbelted white robe with BC (for Bart Claus) monogramed on the wide lapel. It had been a gift from Sera. Marencourt came toward him, but halted in his tracks and gave him a wry once-over. Santa stopped even with him and tugged his robe closed. "Were the case files I asked for pulled?"

"Of course. They are ready for viewing. Liam Easton. Sam Follett, or I should say the entire Follett family and Lakeisha Crenshaw. I doubt you'll get through more than those three tonight." The CAE sniffed. "You smell like coconut."

"I know," Santa agreed. "It's the oil Bori uses. It makes me want a piña colada."

Marencourt looked as if he was trying to decide whether to disapprove or not. "I wouldn't mind one myself."

"Coming," Cassarina said as she approached. She had two piña coladas in hand, one large and one small, each with a pineapple wedge, festive straw and mini umbrella.

"Thank you, Ree," Santa said taking the larger.

"Thank you, Cassarina Topincott," Marencourt said as he took his.

"You are both welcome. Would you enjoy popcorn for the viewing?" she asked Santa.

"That sounds good."

She smiled and trooped off to fetch it.

Marencourt also walked on with a jaunty step. "Good progress today," he said over his shoulder.

Santa lifted a brow. Sometimes he wondered who was really in charge here.

The viewing room was round with a domed ceiling. It was used for more than simple viewing; it was for fully experiencing a subject's life. You could smell what the subject smelled, feel what they felt, understood what they knew. People were complex and it was important to evaluate fairly and comprehend clearly. The naughty/nice list (they still euphemistically referred to it that way) was not mere headings with lists of names beneath. Nor was it a label stamped next to each child's name. Just as he had been graded as a youngster, so was each child. Carefully. Fairly.

No child was all nice or all naughty; they were a natural mixture. No child deserved the proverbial lump of coal on Christmas morning, nor had one ever been left, but no child needed a vast quantity of toys and devices either. It was a disservice to any child to make Christmas solely about getting presents.

Santa settled into one of the comfortable captain's chair and took a sip of his drink. "Begin with Liam," he said.

The viewing room darkened and an image appeared of a six-year-old boy at a small kitchen table writing on a piece of paper. Since the viewing room's wall was curved, the image appeared distorted at first, but it cleared as the scene expanded panoramically. Santa's chair adjusted accordingly to provide the best view. The back lowered several inches and the footrest extended as the seat sunk lower to the floor.

Santa brought the straw to his lips. The straw was expandable, so he did not have to lift the glass. The scene in front of him grew larger and clearer and it became as if he was there. Something savory was cooking. Macaroni and cheese. It bubbled on the stove.

Ree and another elf, Zettle, entered the viewing room with bowls of popcorn, which went on trays on either side of Santa. There was buttered popcorn, caramel corn and cheese popcorn. "Thank you, ladies," Santa said without taking his eyes off the screen.

"You're welcome," they said softly in unison before silently exiting.

In the Easton kitchen, an older boy of seventeen came into the kitchen and went to the stove. He stirred the mac and cheese which had begun to stick to the bottom of the pan.

Santa took in scores of details. The family lived in an apartment and it was warm. It was September. Liam was cute with fair hair. He wore glasses and had an eyepatch on his left eye. He leaned on an elbow frowning over his homework. It was math. Addition. Liam put down his pencil and used his fingers to count.

Tommy, the elder brother, opened a can a tuna, filling the room with a pungent scent as he drained it into the sink. Tommy was handsome with dark hair. He wore jeans and a black t-shirt. He opened a can of peas next and the aromas mingled.

"I hate math," Liam complained.

"Math is like a game," his brother replied as he dumped the canned foods into the mac and cheese.

Liam looked over at him in confusion. "A game?"

"Yeah. There's always an answer," Tommy explained. "But sometimes it's hidden. Kind of like a riddle you have to figure out."

Liam made a face. "Is Dad coming home soon?"

"I think he's working late again," Tommy replied.

"He always works late," Liam grumbled.

"Yeah, well, life is expensive, buddy."

The apartment was not a luxurious one. It was billed as affordable living, but their father, Curt Easton just kept up with expenses. Santa was getting the full picture. Curt had married the very pretty Deana Jones when she became pregnant after they had only been dating a few months. He knew she had another child, Tommy, who was nine at the time. Tommy's father, whoever he was, had never taken responsibility for the boy. Curtis refused to be like that.

There were challenges with the marriage from the beginning. Deana either could not or would not keep a job for any length of time. She had been spoiled as a child and she was lazy with terrible eating and drinking habits. She had been called too pretty for her own good, and maybe she was. She was utterly irresponsible.

Baby Liam, on the other hand, was glorious, and Curt took to fatherhood. He responded to the need in Tommy, as well. The boy deserved a lot better than the mother who neglected him most of time. Everything proved to be more important to Deana than her sons. Soap operas, the games on her phone, going out with her friends. She found a new love interest, a man named Charlie Nunn, when Liam was not yet four, and left her husband and sons after clearing out their checking account and saving account. It had been quite a blow.

Santa held up his hand, freezing the video. He closed his eyes and envisioned a late evening a few months after her departure. Curt, tired from work, paid the babysitter and checked on the kids. Liam was in a toddler bed now and Curt had to squat to adjust the covers around him. Next, he peeked in at Tommy who was already in bed. The light from the hallway hit the boy's face just right and Curt saw the tears on his face. "Hey," Curt said softly. He came further in, but Tommy had already wiped his face with the sheet. "You okay, buddy?"

Tommy nodded.

Curt sat on the side of the bed and brushed the boy's hair back. "Is this about Mom?"

Tommy frowned.

"We'll be okay, Tommy. I promise."

"You're not even my dad," he said miserably.

Curt drew back. "Who said?"

Tommy just looked at him, knowing better.

"I say I am. I'm the dad, you're the older brother, Liam is the younger brother. I was married to your mom. We all live at home …together. Like families do."

It was quiet for several seconds before Tommy spoke again. "Is she ever coming back?"

Curt hesitated and then shook his head. "I don't think so. We're a family of three now."

"What if she comes back and wants to take Liam?"

"I don't think that will happen but, if it does, then we'll fight over it. Go to court. Same as if she wants to take you." He paused. "I can't promise what a judge would do, but I can promise you this much. No one is taking my boys without a fight from me."

Tommy shot into his arms and Curt held him tightly.

Yes, Santa saw it. Felt it. The care and understanding that Curt had given his stepson and that Tommy felt for Liam. The only wealth in the home was love, but it was rich and deep.

Santa continued the scene in the kitchen as Tommy leaned over Liam's work. "Good job, but that one needs to be changed." He pointed at the wrong answer.

Liam used his fingers and did the math again. "Eight?"

"Right."

Liam changed the nine he had written to be an eight.

"Okay. Go wash your hands. Dinner is ready," Tommy added in a corny French accent. Liam popped up and Tommy moved his homework and whisked a tablecloth onto the second-hand table. He set out their plates and glasses of milk. The strains of rock music and the sounds of chairs squeaking across the floor came from above as they began to eat.

"Can I take my eye patch off now?" Liam asked.

"Not until bath time. You know that. We've got to get that weaker eye good and strong."

Liam pushed the last of his peas around. "I hate my eyepatch."

"Hey, it has a job to do. You shouldn't hate something just because it has a job to do. Do you hate the toilet brush because it cleans the toilet?"

Liam giggled.

"I'll bet you anything the toilet brush would rather be a … grooming brush to a beautiful horse."

Liam kept giggling. "Did you ask it?"

"No! Are you crazy? I'm not getting any closer to it than this," he said with an outstretched arm and a swivel of his wrist to pantomime cleaning the toilet bowl.

"How can it talk if its head's in the water?"

Tommy looked thoughtful. "Good point." He laughed. "Was that the last of your homework?"

Liam nodded.

"Good. I'll take a picture and send it to Mrs. Rodgers after dinner. What about your letter to Santa? Did you finish it?"

Liam nodded. "I already sent it. I want a remote-control car. They're so cool."

"They are," Tommy agreed.

"Derek has one, but he won't let anyone else play with it."

"Derek is a jerk."

Liam grinned and then giggled.

"What color car do you want?" Tommy asked.

Liam shrugged.

"What color is Derek's?" Tommy asked with a funny face.

"Red. It has big wheels. He said it cost five hundred dollars."

Tommy snorted. "I doubt that. He just likes to brag."

"Can we play a game after dinner?"

"No can do, little man. I've got my homework and a test to study for. Just because we're all virtual doesn't mean the homework lets up."

"Hey, Tommy?"

"What?"

"When you go to college, what will I do?"

"What do you mean? You'll go to second grade. Hopefully in person. You'll hang out at the Parker's after school and I'll talk to you all the time and see you on weekends."

"I wish you didn't have to go."

"I'll be lucky to go. You know I want to do research. Maybe find a cure to rotten diseases like the Corona virus. First I have to get in, though. I am going to have to get stellar SAT scores and a major scholarship." He got up and took his dishes over to the sink and Liam did the same. "You can go play until your bath."

Liam started to walk out and then doubled back to hug Tommy's waist. They broke apart at the sound of the front door opening and their dad's voice announcing he was home. "Dad," Liam cried happily and took off.

"You're a lucky guy," Tommy called. "We saved you some tuna casserole."

Curt walked into the kitchen with Liam on his back. "Tuna casserole. Yum," he said drolly.

"Can we play a game?" Liam asked his dad.

Carl reached around to poke Liam's side sending the boy into a frenzy of laughter. "Can I eat first?"

A smile played on Santa's lips. "Next," he said.

The image on the screen was now of a portly man, a landlord, and a tenant, a thirty-four-year-old lady with strawberry blonde hair and blue eyes, Beth Follett. They were standing near the front door of a sparsely decorated apartment. She'd been explaining that the company she worked for had shut down. That was the reason she could not pay her rent at the moment, but she was trying to find another job.

"I get that you've had a tough road," the landlord said. "Can't your ex help?"

She wrung her hands. "He says he'd doing what he can, but he's having a hard time, too. He's nine weeks behind with child support."

"You should have his butt hauled into jail. See if that will jog his purse strings open."

Beth Follett's eyes showed the strain of the last months. "If you could just give us a little more time. I swear I will pay."

"I'm really sorry, Ms. Follett, but I got a family to feed. Look, you got to have some people you can go to."

Tears filled her eyes. "I don't. I wish I did."

"Oh, come on. Parents, grandparents, aunties, uncles, cousins. Look, this can't be my problem.

You're a nice lady and I wish I could help you out, but I ain't made of money."

"Isn't this illegal?" she said in desperation. "I lost my job because of the virus."

"It can't be illegal when it's my livelihood. And if it is, sue me. Sorry, but I gotta' take a hard line on this. He reached for the doorknob, antsy to escape. "Be out by the first of the month."

"Mr. Perry, please!"

It did no good. He left, shaking his head. Beth shut the door and slid down it sobbing.

In the hallway, out of their mother's range of sight, two little girls stood biting their lips. Samantha was five and Sierra was three. Santa held up his hand to halt the viewing. He closed his eyes and honed in on Samantha who had asked for help.

She had choppy, light brown hair that she had cut herself. Afterwards, she didn't know why she'd done it. Sierra had red hair, like their mother. Sam looked more like her dad, although he didn't care about them anymore. He said he did, but it was a lie. And now they were going to lose their house.

As the scene continued, Sierra ran to their mother, crying. Sam found it scary and awful to see Mommy cry, but she most hated anyone seeing *her* cry. She pressed against the wall holding her breath to keep the fear and ache trapped inside.

"Enough," Santa said softly. He suddenly knew that the family had gone to a shelter at first. At one point, they had lived in their car for three days. The girls' father had taken the girls in for a few weeks, but Sierra had cried and had fits of rage which she never did. Sam blamed her dad for it and she didn't like her new stepmother. Beth found another shelter for them to stay in and they were still there, but there was a time limit on stays. They only had another two weeks.

Samantha had written to him asking for a home. A tall order, indeed. "A good SAT score and a new home," he murmured. "Next."

Lakeisha Crenshaw was ten and she did not believe in Santa. She lived in the Children's Home of Richmond, Virginia because no family wanted her. Not that she cared. She didn't want them either. She'd thought it so often that sometimes she even convinced herself of it for a while.

She wasn't wanted because she wasn't pretty, her skin was too dark, and she was dumb. But not *one* of those things was her fault. They were her mother's fault and her father's fault. She didn't know who her parents were since she'd been in the care of the state all her life, but it was still their fault.

Santa saw her in a classroom with a dozen other nine and ten year-olds. The children were all spaced apart and they wore masks over their noses and mouths. They were taking a test, but Lakeisha stared out the window bouncing the eraser of her pencil on her nose.

"Keisha," Miss Applegate said from the front of the room, snapping Lakeisha from her reverie.

"What?" the girl answered crossly.

"Concentrate," Miss Applegate reminded her.

Lakeisha rolled her eyes, but went back to the test. She couldn't wait to grow up and not have to answer to anybody. She was going to be an airplane pilot and everyone would stare in awe when she walked through airports. Or maybe she would be a clothes designer. Except she couldn't draw very well.

"Concentrate," Miss Applegate said quietly as she stepped by her. Lakeisha made a face, but she didn't dislike Miss Applegate. She called her Apple-face just to be mean, but the teacher was okay. Her skin was dark, too, but she was pretty. Keisha sometimes fantasized she was her older sister.

Who knew? One day she might even write a note or a card and send it to Miss A. to tell her so. Maybe a Christmas card. Lakeisha had never received a Christmas card in the mail, but it would have been cool to get one, especially one from somebody telling you how much they liked you and that you'd meant something to them.

"Five minutes to finish," Miss Applegate said from the front of the room. When the time was called, the teacher collected the tests and announced that they would move onto something more fun.

"See a movie?" one of the kids said.

"No. We're going to write a letter to Santa."

This was met with groans and laughter.

"Now I realize not everyone believes in Santa. There are several religions that don't celebrate Christmas and, if that's the case for anyone, let me know as I come around and I'll give you a different assignment."

"You going to write a letter to Santa, too?" Marcel asked the teacher.

"I already did."

More laughter.

"What did you ask for?"

The teacher grinned and shook her head. "Not telling."

"I'm not doing that," Lakeisha said. "It's stupid."

"We don't believe in Santa Claus," Darius said. "Only babies believe in Santa Claus."

The teacher shrugged. "Think of it as an easy writing assignment. One that no one will see except Santa."

"Cept you'll see it, right?" Darius asked.

The teacher shook her head. "No, sir."

Lakeisha scoffed. "So we could write something nasty to him."

Josh laughed. "Jump in a lake, Santa," he said. "Hope you and your reindeer crash in a building."

"If that's what you choose to do," the teacher replied, "I can't stop you. I'm sure Santa will know you don't really mean it."

"Come on, Miss A," Marcel said.

"I wrote to Santa once," Emma spoke up. "I got what I wanted, too. It was a paint set. A nice one. It was like fifty dollars."

"Oh, my God," Drew jeered. "You are such a moron."

"No, she is not," the teacher snapped. "Choose to believe or not to. That's your choice. But do not call other people names or make fun of them because they believe differently than you do."

It was quiet in the room because Miss A didn't get mad very often.

"Writing the letter is your assignment. I hoped you would have fun with it, but it's still your assignment. But here's something for you to think about. Why not have a little fun with it? If there is no Santa, no big deal. But what if there is and you don't even ask for what you want? That seems silly to me."

"You going to mail them to the North Pole?" Marcel asked with laughter in his voice.

"Yes."

"You're just going to open them and read them," Lakeisha accused.

"Actually, I'll give you the envelopes and the stamps and you can put them in the mailbox yourself. Nobody except postal workers can touch the mail once a letter has been posted. It's illegal. So. I suggest you write and ask for something that no one else would get you and nobody else would know about."

The kids were still skeptical, but they were softening.

"Get out a piece of paper and get writing. When you're done, we'll get our coats on and take a walk to the mailbox."

A cat, Lakeisha thought bitterly. That's what she'd ask for. She'd found a little gray cat once when she was five and smuggled it into the home of the foster family she was with at the time. The stupid thing had gotten fleas everywhere. The cat had been tossed out and she'd been punished. No one let you have cats in places like that or places like this. She wrote six words. *Santa, I'd like a cat. Lakeisha.* She rolled her eyes and folded up her paper. "Done," she sang.

Miss Applegate sighed. She walked closer and squatted next to her. "Please tell me this is not a two-word message," the teacher said just above a whisper. "With the first word beginning with an F and the second word being 'you.'"

"Oh," Lakeisha said stupidly. "Like forget you?"

"*Mm-hmm*," Miss A said with a nod. "Like that."

"It's not," Lakeisha said. "I asked for something." She paused before adding, "I told you I'd stop saying that other thing."

"Yes, you did." The teacher stood and gently squeezed Keisha's shoulder before she went to her desk for an envelope and a stamp. She brought it back and gave the girl a smile. "Faith, you," she said with a wink.

<u>Chapter Four</u>
The Think Tank

The next morning, the alarm clock went off to the chipper tune of Santa Claus is coming to town. Santa had ordered an alarm for seven a.m., but he hadn't requested the song. Undoubtedly, that was Marencourt's humor at work.

Santa showered, trimmed his beard and mustache, and dressed in his favorite sweats, bright orange with white stripes, and tennis shoes. He had not played tennis in more than fifty years, but he would be getting a different sort of game going today. Santa Claus *was* coming to town and then heading out on his final ride. It was time to get to work. He left his room and made his way to the informal dining room where he breakfasted while making notes. "What I need is a think tank," he mused aloud.

Vestor entered the dining room. "Sir?"

"A think tank," Santa repeated. "A panel of our sharpest thinkers for difficult cases," he mused aloud. "Outside the box thinkers."

"I shall post it at once."

"I'd like to meet with them this morning if at all possible."

"Elves are already volunteering. How many do you wish for? And should there be a qualification to join? Elves are honest by nature, but some may have a higher opinion of their intelligence and creativity than is truly merited."

Santa mulled it over. "Vestor, are elves evaluated?"

"Indeed, Your Majesty."

"Will you sit and have a cup of tea? I'd like to hear it explained."

Vestor gasped softly. His lips quivered and tears filled his wide, lavender eyes. "It would be an honor," he said in a voice choked with emotion. He went to the end of the table, taking his time in order to get himself under control. Santa saw Vestor's silk hanky come out of his pocket and get used to dab his eyes. By the time he sat, Ree was there with tea and crumpets for him. She set it down and gave him a smile of support before leaving again.

Santa finished his muffin stuffed with cranberries and walnuts and slathered in butter.

"Most elves born into a family follow the profession of the household," Vestor began. "Be it bakers or mechanics. Electricians or performers. Librarians or llama keepers. There are thousands of jobs and, as you know, more than three million elves in the city."

Santa nodded.

"But occasionally an elf has different talents. We are all tested in our youth."

"Is it similar to how humans are scored?"

"We undergo more of a vocational and natural ability assessment while humans are scored more on character."

"I see."

"For purposes of your think tank," Vestor said slowly. He took a sip while considering his next words. "You'll want solution finders to complex issues."

Santa nodded. "Precisely that. Well said."

Vestor basked in the moment. "I would suggest elves that have scored highly in problem solving, HCE, *uh*, human current events," he clarified. "Logistics, creativity and empathy."

"Empathy?"

"Yes, sir. Elves score very differently on the empathy chart. Which is perfectly logical. Technicians and plumbers and construction workers don't need a high score. On the other hand, reindeer trainers, any elf in the service industry and elfkin-minders are required to score highly in the category. It's the right of every elf to be happy in their work so we take our calling assessments seriously." He paused before adding, "I suggest a collective score of at least thirty-four for any member of your think tank."

"I'll leave that to you with my full trust, Vestor." Vestor teared up again, so Santa reached for his tea and stirred it unnecessarily to give the HHE time to collect himself. Vestor was a sensitive one. "Will an hour's time be sufficient?"

Vestor merely nodded. He wasn't capable of speaking.

"Let's say in the conference room," Santa added.

Vestor rose, bowed and left.

~~~

An hour later, Marencourt walked with Santa to the conference room. "Your think tank was a sought after assignment," the CAE stated. "Twenty-seven elves have gathered who, by the way, scored a perfect forty. I should not think you will need more than those twenty-seven elves. If only humans would listen and heed their advice, there is a not a problem on earth STT could not solve."

"STT?"

Marencourt gave him a sideways look. "Santa's Think Tank, obviously."

Santa grunted. "I like it."

"Vestor may act as moderator," Marencourt continued. "So long as he can keep his emotions in check," he added with a look of distaste.

Santa's guess was that Marencourt had *not* scored highly in empathy.

"On a different matter," Marencourt said, "the selection committee for the new administration is ready to meet with their recommendations. Will this afternoon at three be convenient?"

"Yes, of course." They were approaching the open door to the conference room. The room hummed with voices and excitement which was nice to hear.

"I suggest you take a power nap after lunch," Marencourt said. "And have a strong cup of tea or coffee before the meeting."

Santa glanced at him curiously, but they had reached the room, so he continued in. "Hello and thank you for joining me," Santa greeted as he went to take his place at the head of the table. "I am delighted to see you all." Around the long table sat elves of various shapes and sizes. He did not recognize them all. "I wonder if we should all introduce ourselves," he suggested cheerfully.

Marencourt had seated himself at the far end of the table and the chair had risen to the optimum height. His forearms rested on the table and his hands lay one over the other. "They all know who you are," he said. "And time is of the essence."

Santa quirked a brow at him. "Fine."

"Shall we jump right into the cases?" Vestor asked.

"Indeed," Santa replied. "Let's do."

"Liam," Vestor said.

The top section of the rectangular walls leaned in to form a wide tray ceiling with each side becoming a screen. The image on each screen was of a smiling Liam.

"Liam is almost seven," Vestor said. "Abandoned by his mother, raised by his father, Curt." A picture of Curt and Liam working a puzzle morphed onto the screens. "And elder half-brother Tommy," Vestor added as the image changed to show Liam and Tommy inside a sheet fort. "Liam originally asked Santa for a remote-control car, which his father can and will get him," Vestor continued. "So will Tommy. The one Tommy purchased for $29.99 is yellow with—"

"Vestor," Marencourt cautioned.

Vestor winced. "Sorry. Later, Liam wrote a second letter to Santa withdrawing his wish and instead asking for Tommy, a senior in high school, to do well on his SATs."

"How do we help this family?" Santa mused, looking around the room.

One elf raised his hand and stood. "I am Foila-Napp, Your Majesty." He was thin with a long nose and small goatee.

"Of the Foila clockmakers," Vestor explained to Santa. "And the Napp tailors, renowned for—"

"Vestor," Marencourt said under his breath.

Vestor clammed up.

"There are preparatory classes," Foila-Napp said. "For college entrance exams. We could arrange for one."

A female elf sitting next to Santa made a face. "But so much is online," she said, looking around the room. "Tommy needs personal coaching," she implored. "All the poor children sitting in front of computers." She looked at Santa and blushed. "I'm Avril from AGW."

"Advanced gift wrap," Vestor supplied quickly.

"A tutor," Santa said. "I like it." He looked at Foila-Napp. "I like the prep class idea, as well. Good thinking."

An elf in middle of the table rose and stood on his chair. "Fizwater, Your Majesty," he introduced with a bow of his head. "It just so happens, there is a lady in their apartment building."

"Yes," another elf exclaimed.

"Catherine Johnson," Fizwater added quickly before another elf did.

An image of a woman in her late fifties came onto the screen as she sat in front of her computer in a virtual teaching session with a young Japanese student. The boy was probably nine or ten. He was reading an original story.

"He decided to stay," the boy read. "His parents did not like it, but there was nothing they could do."

Catherine Johnson smiled and clapped her hands. "Haruto, that was amusing. Good job!" The conversation between the lady and boy went on, but the sound was muted.

"She teaches English to students in other countries," Fizwater said. "It's an early morning job. She used to work in an upscale gift shop as well but it shut down because of the virus."

"She has degrees in English literature and philosophy," another elf interjected. "She and Tommy would work well together."

"Also, she lives alone," Avril said. "She's has a daughter and grand-daughters that she hasn't been able to see for months except on electronic devices. Helping Tommy and perhaps Liam would help her, as well."

Santa nodded. "Good. Can we arrange for her to tutor Tommy?"

"It can be done," Marencourt replied. "Volunteers?"

Hands shot up and he chose three of them with a wave of his finger.

"Plus a prep course," Santa said. "The best that can be had. And for Liam," he said slowly.

"What about magnetic blocks," an elf suggested.

"A cool tent," Vestor suggested. "He loves tents."

"Another remote-control car?"

"Yes," Santa replied with a pleased smile. "To all of them."

"Next case," Marencourt said.

~~~

"Awaken me after a fifteen minute nap," Santa said. *If I can sleep*, he thought. The think tank had been productive as far as ideas, but would the solutions prove to be successful? They'd gone through eight of his more difficult cases and the key to some of them involved another person or even a chain of them. It is not normally how they worked.

An elderly man by the name of Charles F. Fuller was one of the biggest question marks. He was a seventy-five-year-old resident of Indianapolis, the same city as the Folletts. He was alone in the world, having lost his wife and son decades ago, but he was determined to stay in his home for the rest of his days.

He needed assistance and company, even though he would not ask for it. Beth, Samantha and Sierra needed a home and they had assistance and company to offer. How to pair them up was the question.

A direct contact visit had been suggested. Marencourt did not care for the idea, but he could not overrule it if Santa was in favor. A direct contact visit was a rare thing, practically non-existent, but it could work. Or it could backfire. What if Charles had a heart attack from the shock of it? What if he became convinced he had lost his mind or some such thing? The man was desperately lonely and talked to himself quite a bit. What if he thought he'd gone round the bend?

Santa watched the dancing stars on the ceiling of his sleep dome. He slept each night in bed, but he napped in this fully enclosed, softly vibrating unit. The top of it was merely a hand reach away, but it appeared much further. It was as if he was peering at the night sky.

His other concern was Lakeisha. Would her gift be enough? She needed hope. She needed to believe in herself. So did most of the children in orphanages and foster homes. "What would you say, my love?" he whispered. He closed his eyes. "Sera."

<u>Chapter Five</u>
The Successor

The selection committee was assembled and seated in the conference room when Santa arrived, although they stood upon his entry. The table was smaller than earlier in the day, a wide oval. This was a solemn group, utterly different from the youth and vibrancy of STT. There were twelve of them, including Marencourt, none younger than five-hundred-fifty-two years of age. They were resolute in their charge, proud of their heritage, and firm in their convictions. They sat a few feet apart from one another in high-necked robes and headgear.

Santa reached his place at the table. "Felicitations to you noble elven lords and ladies," Santa greeted with a bow of his head.

"And to you, Majesty," they responded with a bow.

Santa sat and they followed suit, all except for the committee chair, Thaunsmoore Christoffian, an elf of eight hundred plus years who stood toward the middle of the table. "On this auspicious occasion," he began in a rusty voice.

Most of the elves stared straight ahead, expressionless, but Marencourt's impatience could be felt from the other end of the table.

"As we," Thaunsmoore continued with a slow sweep of his hand, "gathered here, choose a successor." He paused a long moment. "On this, the eve of the setting of the sun of one reign and the dawn of another."

Marencourt gave a muffled squeak in his throat. He looked to be in agony.

"Let us pay homage to those who have gone before," Thaunsmoore Christoffian said.

"He has the history books," Marencourt said, unable to restrain himself. "Can we just get to it?"

Every head turned to him with looks of staunch disapproval. The eldest female, Mare-Eustophia, spoke saying, "It is tradition, Marencourt."

"Homage should be paid," Objurian of the Creedmir Toymakers added.

"Then may we, at least, begin with the human modern age?" Marencourt insisted.

All heads turned to Thaunsmoore Christoffian who was still on his feet and looking a bit wobbly. The ancient elf gave a small wave of concession.

"And perhaps Vestor could name them," Marencourt added. "Being that time is of the essence."

"So be it," the committee chair said as he sat with all the dignity he could muster with his bones creaking and while stifling involuntary grunts of discomfort.

Vestor came into the room and bowed.

"Proceed, Vestor," Marencourt said. "The abbreviated version if you please."

Vestor clasped his fingers together in front of him. "Quintus Octavius and his wife Valeriana served admirably from the year 171 A.D." He paused and glanced at Marencourt to see if that was sufficiently abbreviated. Marencourt's brows quirked as he considered. "Antoine Descartes served capably from 229 A.D," Vestor continued. "As did his wife Nezot."

Marencourt gave a circular wave of his finger, meaning speed it up.

"Nicholas of Bari served in a most spirited fashion from 287 A.D."

"A firebrand," Bertikin Foursquare murmured despairingly. He was seated to Santa's immediate left.

"From that point on, all Claus's were stationed here on a fulltime basis," Vestor added.

Santa knew this, of course. Nicholas, widely known as Saint Nicholas, made such a name for himself in his day that he was still well-known today. In fact, to many people, the names Santa Claus and St. Nick were synonymous.

"Next, from the kingdom of Ireland, came Feidhlim of Kildare and his wife Ita who served—" Vestor continued.

"And then there was Miguel de la Barca and wife," Marencourt interrupted. "Who took charge in 465."

"George Marsden," Vestor said, speaking just as rapidly. "And wife Camille, a true beauty, came here in 523 and was—"

"John of the Cross, 581," Marencourt interrupted again.

"Nobuyuki," Vestor said. "And his wife—"

All heads had turned to the duo who were not even allowing the other to finish, going faster and faster. A dozen set of eyes dance back and forth between the elves as names, dates and occasional comments blurred together.

"In the year 813—"

"Senebi of Cairo and his—"

"Herbert the third."

"His reign was cut short—"

"—was inducted in ten forty-five 1045."

"Now she was special."

"Sir John Miller—"

'In 1219, Saul of—"

"—who became the second Canadian to—"

"—and his third wife, Anne."

"Lyudmil Covaci—"

"In 1535, Michel de Nostredam was chosen—"

"William Fisher and his wife Hannah followed and—"

"Ivan the fair—"

"Phillip Lamarck and his—"

"—began in 1741."

"Simonson's reign was cut short by—"

"—and his second wife, Bea."

"Eighteen fifty-seven was—"

"And then there was Manfred Delamont, your predecessor, an Englishman whose reign began in 1915," Vestor concluded. "His wife was affectionately called Dolly. Their tenure went as well as could be expected given two world wars and other factors."

Santa nodded soberly. He had been honored to train with the man, and Mrs. Dolly Claus had taken Sera under her wing.

"So here we are today," Marencourt said. He nodded to Vestor who promptly left the room. "You have not experienced this side of events," Marencourt continued, directing it to Santa. "But it is quite simple, really. We have selected the finest candidates and narrowed them down to groupings that you will be presented in groups of twelve. We shall begin with the most promising group."

A rectangle shape on the table in front of Santa rose several inches exposing a lid that flipped up to reveal a screen. On the screen were a dozen black and white photographs in three lines of four.

"These first twelve are in no certain order," Marencourt said. "Touch on any picture to get a full report."

Santa cocked his head in puzzlement. "Why are there women on here?"

The female elves in the room bristled. "Why not?" Marta-dame Gildenfinger snapped.

He was incredulous. "For Santa Claus?"

"As I believe you well know," Theodoppolis Doppleside spoke up. "Any human that sees Santa Claus, sees what they expect to see."

Santa certainly did know it. The shock of one such experience had nearly stopped his heart.

"Perhaps we *should* have begun with an earlier human era," Marta-dame Gildenfinger opined in a miffed tone. "Santa Claudia?" she exclaimed. "Only one of the most famous Santas of the ancient era. You do know that Santa is the Spanish word for female saint," Marta-dame persisted.

Santa gave a gesture of concession. "I beg your pardon. I meant no offense. I had simply not considered it."

She gave a regal nod of clemency and he went back to studying the screen. The ages of the people in the photographs ranged from thirty to forty for the most part. There was one younger man, in fact, he had quite a baby face, and one older man who had to be sixty. The pictures were not terribly clear which was peculiar for technology as advanced as theirs.

Santa touched the picture of a man with a scholarly look about him. The image enlarged and went in color before a succession of photographs and videos played. On each of the four tray-ceiling screens, the same images were displayed. An audio track provided an overview of the subject.

"Brandon James Tipton. Thirty-nine years of age, married, no children, a collective score of six hundred and eleven. He is a mid-list author of young adult novels married to Emilia Anne Tipton (nee Wilson), an administrator in the local school system. They reside in Lincolnshire and have two dogs that would join them, Camden and Nugget."

Santa stared at the screen blankly. A great deal of information and emotions had come across during the report. Just as in the viewing room, he'd *experienced* the Tiptons. Their feelings, beliefs, likes and dislikes. Their prejudices, mistakes and triumphs. He'd glimpsed their entire lives in a span of some twenty-eight seconds. "Whoa," he said under his breath. He gave a quick shake of his head.

"Headphones are available," Marencourt stated dispassionately. With a flick of his finger, a drawer to Santa's right slid open to reveal a pair of wireless headphones. "You will need them for the non-English speaking candidates."

Santa picked them up while sending a look of disdain Marencourt's way. "It is a lot to take in," he said defensively.

"What did you think of him?" Bertikin Foursquare asked Santa. The elf wore spectacles and peered over the top of them to address others.

"He seemed nice," Santa replied. "They both did. They would be a fine choice."

"But are you *tingling*?" Doppleside asked.

Santa noticed that all the elves were watching him. It was disconcerting. "Tingling?" he repeated.

"Next," Marencourt called.

The image of Brandon James Tipton was whisked away. Santa started to object, but they all knew something he didn't. He directed his attention back to the screen and, in the interest of political fairness, touched the image of a woman. She was attractive with short hair.

As with Tipton, the photograph enlarged and then dozens of other images came up. Sophia. A professor. Divorced. Fluent in three languages. With a small gasp, Santa had a sudden understanding of how good a woman would be in the role. Sophia Levesque was bright, compassionate, organized and a hard worker. She had a wonderful sense of humor and excellent communication skills. "Yes," he muttered. "I see it."

"See it," Marencourt repeated. "But do you feel it?"

Santa considered how to reply. "I never considered a woman in the role. But I see it now. So, yes. I suppose you could say I … feel it."

Jacques Tasselton, to Santa's immediate right, reached over and touched his arm. A moment later he shook his head and Sophia was whisked off the screen.

Santa objected with a huff. "Are you saying I'm going to have some sort of physical reaction? That the tingling is physical? What? Will I vibrate?"

No one answered. They all just looked at him. It was aggravating to be in the dark. "Then why don't I touch them all until I feel it?" he snapped at Marencourt. "You are the one who keeps reminding me that time is of the essence."

"Because you must consider them," Tasselton explained. "Truly cogitate on each of them."

"The choice cannot be made lightly," Doppleside added.

"Indeed not," Marencourt retorted crossly. "The seven thousand, six-hundred and forty nine years of wisdom seated around this table have spent countless hours—"

"Not countless," Kajillian Hemplefoote rejoined. The Hemplefoote's were all peacemakers. "I believe there were thirty-three thousand fourteen hours between all of us."

Mare Eustophia cleared her throat. "I put in three hours more yesterday," she corrected Kajillian.

"Ah," Kajillian said. "Thirty-three thousand seventeen hours," he said to Santa.

Santa frowned as he went back to the screen. He put on the earphones and touched the picture in the top left corner. As the picture got larger and went in color, he realized it was a light-skinned black man with an infectious smile and beautiful brown eyes. Palmer Allard, forty–one years of age. A resident of Paris. Occupation Chef. Wife Camille. They lost their only child, a young son, Andre, to a rare cancer. Palmer Allard was a good, deeply passionate man, but Santa felt no tingle.

Santa closed his eyes and blindly touched the screen. In his mind, he saw a fit, bald man. Axel Haas, thirty-one years of age from the city of Hamburg. A headmaster of a school. No tingle.

He touched blindly again and other images occurred to him. He saw the faces and pictures as clearly as if he'd been staring at the screen. William Cramer and wife Elizabeth. They owned and managed a bakery.

No tingle. Lena Delany, forty years of age, and her husband Phil. She ran an adoption agency. He'd retired from a career in advertising to head up a not-for-profit organization. A strong marriage, good people, but no tingle.

As Santa experienced the candidates, Marencourt made a drinking gesture. Moments later servers bustled in with trays of beverages favored by each committee member. Hot chocolate, eggnog, beer, fizzy water, milkshakes. Marencourt accepted his martini with a frown. "I like extra ol—"

Before he could complete the complaint, Cassarina plunked in a toothpick with extra olives into the glass.

Santa was wondering if he had misunderstood the directive. He was supposed to experience a physical sensation when the right person was presented? He had just seen nine exceptional candidates and had not felt a thing. He could have had confidence in any of them, but he had not felt a tingle. There were only three candidates left in the first dozen. He touched the picture of the old one to get him out of the way. Good golly, if the man didn't look like Santa Claus! Not that it mattered.

Al Dorsett, fifty-eight years of age. From Cleveland, Ohio. Retired.

A throbbing jolt went through Santa causing him to gasp. His eyes bulged. The old man? The old man was the one? Santa couldn't concentrate on the report for the gyration making him pulsate as if a low-voltage electric current was running through him. He looked around and found all eyes on him. It looked like their breaths were collectively held. Tasselton reached out and gingerly touched him and then jerked back with a happy squeal. A moment later, nearly all of the committee was on their feet, most of them applauding and cheering.

The voltage (*that* was what they had called a tingle?) subsided. Thank Heaven. It had been just shy of painful.

"I told you," Marta-dame Gildenfinger gloated to the much shorter, suddenly scowling, Zicarian Missleschwitz standing next to her. Her hand jutted out. "Pay up."

He gave her a sour look but raised his hand, fisted it and plunked perfect red rubies into her open palm.

The old man of the group, Santa thought with a shake of his head. He was flabbergasted. A feeling of pure joy filled the air, but Santa was not sharing it. Marencourt, the only elf who had not risen, smiled and lifted his glass to Santa. Santa grunted, not that it was heard over the majestic sounding music that had begun playing to the tune of *Land of Hope and Glory.*

The committee members began singing, all except Marencourt who was enjoying his martini, but even he waved his hand and swayed with the music.

Man of hope and glory, father of love and glee.

How shall we adore thee, we who proudly serve thee?

Brighter still and brighter, are the prospects now set.

God made thee mighty. Make thee mightier yet! God made thee mighty, make thee mightier yet!

The chairelf, Thaunsmoor Christoffian, raised his hand and the others sat again. "A successor is named," he called, as was tradition. Now, besides joy and excitement filling the air, there was the sound of distant bells. Throughout the city, bells of every shape and size were being rung. Handbells, bells in steeples, doorbells, the small bells mounted to animal harnesses.

A dignified-looking photograph of the successor showed on all the ceiling screens with the caption 'Dortsett-Claus January 10, 2021-January 8, 2079.'

Replaced, Santa thought with unexpected resentment. By an old man who looked more like Santa Claus than he did. And he was Santa Claus, damn it!

His personal viewing station had retreated back into the table. As Thaunmoore began the laborious process of sitting again, all attention was riveted on the now-larger screens. "Alfred," Vestor said from behind Santa, causing him to jump since he hadn't noticed the HHE come back into the room, much less walk over to stand behind him. Santa turned to scowl at him.

"I do beg your pardon, Your Majesty," Vestor apologized.

Santa faced front again. Was Marencourt smirking?

"Alfred Tennyson Dorsett," Vestor began again. "Born February third, nineteen sixty-two."

That meant the old man had been in diapers when he and Sera had been named the successors. It was a peculiar thought. An image of baby Al appeared followed by a photograph of the young boy he'd grown into. Next came an image of him as a young man. In the fourth picture, he was in his mid-twenties and wearing a tuxedo as he posed next to his blushing bride.

"An excellent student," Vestor continued. "His educational path veered toward philosophy and the sciences. He earned an advanced degree in astrophysics before accepting a professorship. Married for twelve years until his wife Carolyn passed away from a brain aneurism."

A wave of compassion rolled over Santa. He knew the toll of the loss of a beloved wife.

A video clip began of Al's interview. In it, he sat in a red leather chair, the same chair in the same room that all the prospects had been in for their PSI (preliminary Santa interview.) Al wore a pale blue, crew-neck sweater. "It was a dark time," Al said. "Or, rather, the dark time came after, because Carolyn's death was so sudden. She went to dress for work after breakfast and collapsed. I was walking out the door when I heard the fall." He paused and shook his head. "Who knows why such things happen? But the shock of it, the reminder of how short life is, caused me to reevaluate and to change course."

Another image of Al in the dress robes and cap of a professor during convocation was momentarily displayed. "I went," Al said, "from being a professor at a prestigious university to teaching seventh grade science." He slapped the air in front of him and laughed uproariously. "Absurd! That's what they all said. But, you see, I wanted to engage with younger minds, to ignite youngsters' curiosity about the universe and all its wonders." Still grinning, he added, "Do you know I had to go back for more education? They let me teach those first few years by way of what they called *lateral* entry." He laughed again. "From a PhD of astrophysics to a middle-school science teacher. But there were education courses to tick off the list and so I did."

"Did you regret the decision?" asked the interviewer who was off screen.

"No. Never. I taught for thirteen wonderful years before moving into administration, and then I was a principal of an elementary school for another sixteen years. No, I never regretted it. I loved it. Those are the minds and lives you can touch and help shape."

"Why did you leave it?"

"I only just left last year. It was before the pandemic hit. I left because I wanted to write a book about keeping the passion for teaching alive. But writing is hard work. I'd written academic papers over the years, but the book languished. I missed my students and staff and the daily work. Of course, then the isolation of Covid began."

On the screens came an image of Al dressed as Santa in an impressive costume.

"Tell us about playing Santa," the interviewer said.

"It was a highlight every year," he replied. "I grew out the beard for three months beforehand. I even bought my own Santa suit. The suits you can rent are so lackluster." He smiled at a memory. "Naturally, my students saw me at school during that time. Let's face it; I look like Santa even in regular clothing, but with the beard and mustache …every year I got asked if I *was* Santa, as in the real deal."

"What did you say?"

"I told them the real Santa was my brother," he replied gleefully. "That's why I look so much like him. Obviously, my brother, Nick, lives in the North Pole. I even had a picture concocted which I kept in my office. It was me in my Santa suit next to me in a sweater and jeans. It looked as though I was standing next to my brother."

"You had no children of your own," the interviewer said.

The smile on Al's face faded. "No. It wasn't to be. We had begun the process of hopefully adopting when—"

There was a brief silence before the interviewer spoke again. "And what of Mrs. Claus?"

"Mrs. Claus? Are you referring to CJ?" Al must have gotten an affirmative reaction, because he said, "CJ played Mrs. Claus alongside me for the last nine years."

The image on the screen switched to one of an attractive middle-aged lady with reddish brown hair. The next photograph was her in a Mrs. Claus costume, complete with a white wig. The next was of her seated next to Al in the role of Santa. They sat on throne like chairs and stared adoringly at one another.

"Cynthia is her name," Al said. "Cynthia Jo Walters, but she's always gone by CJ. She is a lovely person and a dear friend."

"Who was widowed three years ago," the interviewer said.

Al was back on screen and his face flushed. "Yes," he replied guardedly.

"You had cared for her for years."

"In a proper fashion," he said defensively. "Yes."

"And she cared for you."

"Again, in a proper fashion. We are friends. Dear friends."

"But you wanted more."

"I … we—" Al was suddenly tongue tied and flustered. "At a certain point in time," he said haltingly. "One chooses *not* to put friendship at risk."

"Was it not simply a lack of courage?"

He seemed stumped by the question and then his face cleared. Now, he looked sheepish. "Absurd to have a lack of courage at my age, isn't it? I mean, really, what is there to fear except the painful bite of rejection? And she would have been kind about it." He smiled tenderly. "She is the loveliest lady in the world."

"What if you were chosen to be the next Santa Claus?"

He sobered. "I cannot imagine the privilege."

The screen went dark. Santa didn't particularly want to like the man but he did.

"The choice has been made," Marencourt said to Santa. "Care for a drink?" He lifted his glass. "These are excellent."

"Make mine a double," Santa replied as the bells continued to ring.

BOOK II: THE CHOSEN

Chapter Six
Al

S anta stood in front of his wardrobe in his boxers, undershirt and socks, contemplating the right outfit to wear. There were seven days until Christmas Eve, and Alfred Tennyson Dorsett was expected to arrive in the next few hours. The inheritor. The successor. The chosen.

Of all the candidates, Al was now the only one who remembered being approached, interviewed and offered the position. The others' memory of the same events had been erased. They would be left to wonder where the chunk or chunks of gold in their possession had come from. Al's official contract would be signed once he was in residence but he had gleefully agreed to the arrangement.

The way the initial NPTC (North Pole to candidate) contact worked was through a dream visitation from Santa himself explaining that the dreamer was being considered for the role of a Claus. So that they would know the vision was true and actual, they were told they would experience the same dream for three consecutive nights. And so they did.

On the third night, they were instructed where to find a token of North Pole esteem, a nugget of gold, and told that if they wished to decline further consideration, (understanding that their human existence would be erased if they were chosen) they could keep the gold along with the very best wishes from all the occupants of the North Pole.

If, on the other hand, they wanted to remain a contender, they were to place the nugget under their pillow which opened the way for a direct contact visit and the first interview. And so it had occurred as foretold.

Santa selected a gray sweater from the wardrobe and then changed his mind. He would not wear gray. Next he pulled out a black turtleneck, but quickly stuck it back. Not gray and not black, for goodness sake. He would meet the incumbent today and make a good and colorful first impression. He would begin training and advising Al Dorsett and he would do it admirably, as was his obligation.

He pulled on a red turtleneck and a bright blue sweater with flying reindeer on it. A bit of whimsy was the ticket. A pair of black trousers completed the outfit. "Showtime," he said to his image in the mirror before striding from the room.

"Well," Marencourt said when they met in the corridor. "Don't you look … comfy. No formal attire to meet the next in line?"

"He will see me in formal attire soon enough. Until then, there is work to do. Only seven days until the big night."

"Why, thank you! That knowledge is so useful since I had—" He sharply cocked his head. "Had I forgotten?" He paused dramatically before finishing. "No."

"I need an update," Santa said pleasantly. He was determined not to get ruffled today. He was in charge today.

Marencourt fell in step with him. "Things are well in hand. The superfluous gift request period has ended and the last of the presents are headed to giftwrap. Logistics has completed this year's route and—"

"I meant an update on my cases."

"Things have begun," Marencourt replied carefully. "STT is busily working on every facet. You might want to take your protégé to the viewing room for an update later."

"Protégé," Santa repeated wryly.

"Protégé, apprentice, trainee, replacement, the next Santa, whatever you want to call him." An assistant to Marencourt approached with a shiny booklet which he passed to Marencourt and Marencourt then passed to Santa with the explanation, "The training curriculum."

Santa and Marencourt came to a halt while the assistant walked on. Santa glanced through the booklet, thirty pages of small writing which listed everything the new Santa needed to know in exhaustive detail under headings of Overview, History, Philosophy, Procedure, Duties, Timelines, Tools, Rules and Restrictions, Protocol, Key Personnel, Maps with guides, and FAQs.

"It is rather condensed," Marencourt said, "because we are getting a late start."

Santa felt a twinge of guilt at the reminder.

"You will recall that young fellow Bart and his wife Sera had three and half weeks with the Claus's before Christmas Eve."

"I do remember," Santa said with a humility that seemed to take the CAE aback. "And I am truly sorry I dropped the ball these last months. I owed a responsibility that I did not live up to. Sera would be disappointed in me. I am disappointed in myself."

Marencourt frowned. He did not like being put in the role of consoler. "For the most part, you have made up for it, but it will be a fast-paced training schedule." He sighed and reached out to touch Santa's arm and pat it. "There there."

Santa guffawed. "Empathy is not your strong suit. Am I right?"

Marencourt took back his hand. "We should go to the station."

"A moment, please," Santa said. "To make certain I understand correctly, this is the information he needs to know."

"Yes."

"But the manner in which he receives the information is not stipulated."

"Correct. Other than quickly. I would suggest concentrating on this final phase of preparation and the big event itself. You'll have until the tenth of January to cover the less critical matters."

Santa murmured his understanding and strode forward with a brisk step and lighter heart. Confession really was good for one's soul. He felt unburdened.

"I do not know if you recall how disorienting that first teleportation is—" Marencourt warned.

"Of course I do. Poor Sera felt as though she was walking sideways. I kept a tight grip on her but the truth is that I felt it myself. Everything felt stilted for an hour or more."

"Common reaction," Marencourt replied.

"I realize—" Santa broke off and came to abrupt halt. "Al Dorett. AD. I just realized. My informal initials are BC, Bart Claus, and his are AD. How funny!"

"Hilarious," Marencourt said dryly. He motioned onward and they began walking again. "You were saying?"

"I realize the fellow will need to rest for the first few hours. Then perhaps we could have a light luncheon followed by—"

"Chief," came a tinny, disembodied voice.

Marencourt swiped the air and a hologram of Phinsmith, one of the station engineers, appeared before them. "Yes? What is it?"

"He is here," Phinsmith said breathlessly. "Ahead of schedule. He refused any sedation and was ready and eager to go. We had a good headwind and—"

"We're on our way," Marencourt replied.

"I mean to say we are *here.*"

Marencourt and Santa stopped again. "Here … where?" Marencourt asked.

"The south corridor."

"We're nearly there," Santa said. "Is he walking without aid?"

"I wouldn't say *walking* exactly," Phinsmith replied haltingly.

The baffled Santa and the CAE continued forward, rounded the corner and stopped to see Al Dorsett coming toward them – dancing toward them was a more fitting description. The man was giddily stepping, waving his arms about as he looked around. He seemed nearly delirious. When Al Dorsett saw Santa, he stopped with a gasp. "Oh," he cried and his eyes filled with tears.

"Hello," Santa said warily.

"Oh," Al said again. He came forth with his hands outstretched.

"He's not going to hug me, is he?" Santa asked Marencourt under his breath.

Marencourt quirked a bushy brow in disapproval of Al Dorsett's lack of decorum.

Al stopped a yard away and bowed. Straightening, he said. "It is such an honor." Tears slipped down his face which he hurriedly wiped away. "I am … overwhelmed."

"Yes, well, you'll get over that," Santa assured him agreeably. "It is good to meet you, Alfred Tennyson Dorsett. May I introduce you to the chief administrative elf of the manor, Marencourt."

"Marencourt," Al repeated. "I am honored to make your acquaintance." He bowed again.

Santa gave a little shake of his head. "Technically, you don't bow to elves except —"

"Eh," Marencourt interrupted while lifting his arms in acceptance of the homage.

Santa barely restrained himself from rolling his eyes. "I congratulate you on the appointment," he said to Al. "It is as wonderful as you might have imagined."

Al pressed his hands to his chest and looked as he might burst into noisy sobs. "Thank you."

"I must say, you have come through teleportation flawlessly," Santa marveled. "Some people feel as if they can't walk straight."

"So did I! But I did a few cartwheels and it fixed me right up."

"Cartwheels. *Hmm*. Can't say I thought of that."

"And you had no sedation," Marencourt commented.

"No, Lord Marencourt," Al said with a shake of his head.

"You don't need to call him—" Santa began.

"Eh," Marencourt said with a shrug, clearly enjoying the adulation.

"I did not want to miss a thing," Al continued. "Not a single moment. I was *fllllown* here. In a blaze of … what is the word?"

"Teleportation," Marencourt replied dryly.

"It was magic. I was there and then I was flying and then I was here. And now I am here. And you are here," he said to Santa. Next he looked adoringly at Marencourt. He whirled around and put his hands on his head.

Santa and Marencourt exchanged a glance. "Indeed," Santa said.

"Breakfast?" Marencourt suggested.

Al turned back around, his face alight. "Yes, please!"

It took more time than usual to get to the dining room because Al was agog at everything he saw. The rooms they passed, elves they encountered, the chandeliers, the winding crystal escalator, the hidey-holes that doll-like scatterkins congregated in to wave and chirp greetings to the new Santa. Every single thing delighted him. The portraits and paintings and tapestries on the wall. The thick carpets and flickering lanterns and enormous hearths with fires blazing. The instrumental Christmas music playing, the coffered ceilings with inlaid gilding. Everything. Finally, they reached the informal dining room.

"I will take my leave," Marencourt said. "And look forward to learning of your progress later." With a bow of his head, he continued down the corridor.

"Until then," Al called.

Santa motioned his protégé into the room and then followed. A round table was set for two, the center of it filled with bowls and platters and plates of food. Piping hot sausages, flapjacks, pastries, hash, eggs, kippers, fruit, bacon, oatmeal, biscuits and gravy.

"It's a welcome feast," Al cried.

"It's breakfast," Santa said. As they sat, Cassarina appeared with a tray of beverages. Santa had his usual, a glass of cold milk and a cup of hot coffee. Al accepted orange juice, coffee and milk, each with profound thanks. "This is Cassarina," Santa said by way of introduction.

"Cassarina," Al repeated. "What a pretty name."

Ree curtsied and then hurried off, blushing. Santa stopped himself from growling deep in his throat. Wasn't the man just the consummate charmer?

"This food," Al exclaimed. He oohed and ahhed over every bite.

Al's pleasure in the meal was distracting. Admittedly, the food was delicious. Had he forgotten just how delicious?

"I have so many questions," Al said between bites. "And I want to know everything about you."

"In time. But there are basics to get through first."

"I will be your most avid student. Where *shall* we begin? I've never wanted to jump into anything as much in my entire life. And that's saying something!"

Santa considered the question as he drummed his fingers on the training booklet. "Vestor," he said. Al looked curious, but then Vestor walked into the room. He stopped with a gasp to see the men sitting together.

"What an honor," the HHE exclaimed. He bowed deeply to Al.

"Al, this is Vestor," Santa said. "Vestor, meet Al Dorsett."

"The incumbent," Vestor said reverently. "Welcome!"

"Thank you, Vestor. You are so tall for an elf," he said with wonder.

"Human-height," Vestor explained. "For the comfort of your kind. Although there are elven professions in which height is an enormous benefit."

"How fascinating," Al said. "I had no idea."

"Vestor," Santa said. As Vestor turned to him, Santa had an inkling he had been forgotten for a moment. "Can the material he needs to know be implanted in his mind?" Santa asked tapping the booklet.

Vestor blinked. "All at once?"

Santa thought about it. Al was a scholar who loved learning. He'd take in information easily. He would also question and chat and share and one topic would segue to another when time was so very limited. "Yes."

"He has the capacity," Vestor replied reluctantly. "But he will need to sleep afterwards. For at least twelve hours."

Santa pressed his fingers together. "I propose this is what we do," he said to Al. "We'll take a brief tour of the manor next."

"Wonderful!"

"And have lunch followed by a quick trip to the summer sanctuary."

"The summer sanctuary!"

"Or perhaps an aerial view of the city. Then we'll let you get settled into your rooms—"

"My rooms," Al said wistfully. His eyes filled, which caused Vestors's lavender eyes to fill as well.

"Then we'll meet for drinks in my office, go over the contract one last time, you'll sign it, we'll have an early dinner and then—" He paused and looked pointedly at Vestor.

"The implantation will be made ready," Vestor replied.

Santa liked the plan. "You can retire about seven or eight," he said to Al, "—have the information you need implanted in your mind—"

"It does not hurt," Vector interjected with a gentle smile at Al.

"And tomorrow, you will know it all and we'll begin anew. We'll go over the letters from this year and visit the main annex and Fenland Forest, if you like."

Al stood, bursting with vigor. "I'm ready!"

Santa chuckled at the man's enthusiasm. "If you don't mind, I'd like to finish my coffee first."

"Of course." Al sat back down and lifted his own cup of coffee in a toast.

Vestor continued to stand there looking hopeful and fidgety. "Would you like to come with us for the tour?" Santa asked.

"If I can be of any help. I am an excellent tour guide, Your Majesty."

"I know you are. I might even learn a thing or two myself."

Vestor beamed.

Chapter Seven
Santa's Manor

A brief tour of the manor could been conducted in a few hours, but they had not yet been through half of it when Santa realized it was past time for lunch. It was a good thing Al was having the vital information implanted because, at the rate they were going, it would months to teach him everything.

Al was curious about everything and everyone and, through his incessant questioning, Santa had learned quite a bit. He had not known Vestor's full name was Vestorias Amourato Haw-Nelter or that Vestor had two brothers and five sisters all of whom worked in hospitality with the exception of his brother Bonjovial who was an aspiring musician and music teacher. Santa felt contrite he'd never asked this information himself.

Nor had Santa known that the yellowish stones in the great bakery hearth had been hand-selected and teleported from a castle in Bavaria in the year twelve-ninety-six, although that didn't seem like terribly important knowledge.

"Lunch, I think," Santa suggested. "There is a café down the way." Not only was it close but the bistro, with its floral motif and pink and white striped tablecloths, specialized in a cheese soufflé he was particularly fond of.

Clearly, he had underestimated the time involved in a tour of the manor, especially for a first-timer. Had he actually forgotten how large the place was? So far, they had visited a side vestibule, the drawing room, the grand salon, the chapel, the staff bakery, the staff cafeteria, the fitness room, the morning room, the atrium, the botanical garden and the library.

Still to go were the kitchens and larders since Al wanted to see them, the office, the private study, the wine cellar, the ale cellar, the music hall, the servant's hall, the game room, the indoor pool, the viewing room, the spa and the residential halls. What was he forgetting? Oh, yes. The tailor's shop. And The Manor Workshop. And probably a dozen other rooms.

They sat at a round table in the café and ordered. The soufflé and a Sauvignon Blanc for him, a club sandwich, onion rings and a root beer for Al, and bean-spouts and tofu for Vestor along with mineral water. "Maybe we should go to the viewing room after this," Santa said, "and do a virtual tour of the manor. Then we can take Nipst for a quick aerial observation of the city."

"Nipst?" Al asked as their drinks were served on a floating tray.

"The North Pole Sky Tram," Santa replied.

"Oh! Fabulous."

"It is rather," Santa agreed. It had been years since he'd ridden it. Why, when they had always enjoyed it so? Their food arrived and they ordered dessert before tucking into the meal. Grasshopper pie for him with coffee, a maple shortbread cookie for Al (the scent was mouthwatering) and lime sorbet for Vestor, who seemed to be having the time of his life.

It was impossible not to notice the staring of elves as they lunched, although most looked away when he looked at them. Others waved or made gestures of victory.

Victory. *Hmm. We shall see.*

"The food," Al marveled.

"Yes," Santa murmured. "It is a perk."

~~~

"Whoa," Al breathed when he walked into the viewing room. "How cool is this?" he said taking in the domed ceiling.

Santa found it amusing that the word cool was still as prevalent as it was. Most of the slang terminology from his day had dried up and blown away like so much dust. No one had it 'made in the shade' anymore. No one said, 'neato' or 'far out.' In fact, on his bi-annual HCEU (human current events update,) he was continually surprised by the day's customs and language and technology. It seemed to him that, these days, people commonly talked in acronyms and they looked more at their handheld devices than at one another. So the continued use of the word cool gave Santa the warm fuzzies.

Al sat at the far end of the three captain's chairs and Santa took the middle seat.

"Comfortable," Al murmured.

"The virtual tour we're about to see is new," Vestor said proudly as he sat in his chair. "I've only seen it once myself." He paused before saying, "Virtual tour of Santa's Manor please. In American English."

Al leaned forward to address him. "Are there many languages to choose from?"

"Oh, yes. All six thousand, five hundred and three of them. Including Elvish."

"Elvish," Al repeated with his eyes aglow. "Would I be permitted to learn Elvish?"

Vestor was moved by the request. "I would think so, although it does take time."

"Could it be implanted?"

Santa was turning his head back and forth with the flow of conversation. He felt a squeeze of remorse that he had never asked to learn the language.

"I'll find out," Vestor pledged, "although, as I said, it would take some time. It takes our young fourteen years to become fully proficient."

"Really?"

"There are many nuances," Vestor explained.

"Ah."

"Shall we?" Santa said, gesturing to get on with it.

The room darkened and their chairs began to adjust. Al giggled which made Santa grin. Vestor beamed with pride.

"Santa's Manor," the silky-voiced narrator said. A mansion loomed in front of them as if they were flying toward it making them all cry out. Al and Vestor both grabbed Santa's arm. The camera moved slightly side to side as if strapped to a great bird, making Santa dizzy. The camera approached and then circled the mansion causing them to sway in their chairs. What a magnificent place it was with its glittering white stone, red-slate many-gabled roofs and ornate windows.

"Construction," the announcer continued, "began in the human era known as the Bronze Age and continued for the next fifteen centuries. The architecture is Châteauesque. There are nearly three hundred thousand square feet of living space shared by Santa, his wife and four hundred and sixteen members of staff."

Santa cringed at the words *his wife* for his own sake and for Al since he didn't have a wife. That was a disadvantage of enormous proportion. How he would have managed without Sera by his side, he did not know. The camera completed a full circle of the mansion and moved toward the front door, which opened in invitation.

"Inside," the voice continued, "there is much to see."

They were now inside the breathtakingly beautiful Grand Entry Hall. It was hexagonal with crystal pillars and a glass roof. In the center of the Entry Hall was a twenty-foot crystal statue of him with his hand raised in a wave. Vestor halted the presentation with a lift of a finger and leaned forward to speak to Al. "The arms of your chair can hug you if you desire."

Al removed his hand from Santa's arm, only just then realizing he'd been clutching it.

"Just wish for it," Vestor said.

Al gave him a quizzical look but then he closed his eyes and the arms of his chair puffed up, softened and closed around him. Al smiled and nodded at Vestor and turned back to the screen, ready for more of the adventure. As the tour continued, the arms of Vestor's chair arms puffed and closed in around him. Santa was tempted to follow suit but was it dignified? *Oh, what the heck,* he thought and his chair snuggled him in a cozy hug.

"There are three hundred and thirty five rooms in the manor, including three kitchens, the informal dining room, the breakfast room, the formal dining room, the banquet hall, a ballroom—"

Each room was shown as it was named. In the more extravagant rooms, the camera took a 360 degree view.

"A favorite destination for any visitor is The Manor Workshop. Located next to Dakina-Carmella's Carmel Apples and Confections, and The Manor Frozen Treats Shoppe, you can allow your nose to happily lead the way."

The scents filled the room and made their mouths water, although all of them were still full.

"In The Manor Workshop, classic toys are made. Colorful wooden blocks and spinning tops, Golly Dolly Dolls, Teddy bears, toy trucks and wooden puzzles. Their signature line of toy reindeers, each the likeness of a flying-team member, is a perennial favorite."

Santa was absorbed in the show, until he was distracted by what felt like his right earlobe being tugged. He looked accusingly at Vestor, but then noticed Marencourt standing behind him. The CAE motioned for him to come. Santa shrugged off the chair snuggle and left the room. "What is it?" he asked in the corridor.

"There appears to be a fungal infection amongst the reindeer affecting their paws."

"All of them?" Santa asked worriedly.

"No, but at least three of them."

"Which three?"

"Fulsome, Danemaster and Donner Junior."

"Oh dear."

"It's likely we will need to pull replacements from the second string."

Santa clucked his tongue. "I hate that. I know how they look forward to the flight. I'll go to them at once."

Vestor stepped from the viewing room and the door sealed shut behind him. "Do you need my help?"

"No, stay with AD, will you?"

"Of course, Your Majesty."

"Continue the tour for as long as he likes. I don't know how long I'll be."

"Shall we take in the city, if he feels up to it?"

"Yes. I'll join you if I can."

"I expect transport-lag to hit sometime soon," Vestor commented. "He may want to sleep the rest of the day."

"Understandable. If we don't meet back up today, tell him we'll breakfast at eight."

"I shall. Give my love to the reindeer?"

"Of course I will," Santa said.

Chapter Eight
Reindeer Paws

S anta led the way to the widest pillar in the corridor. He touched it and the marble casing slid open to reveal a glass and brass tube inside. The door to the tube opened and Santa stepped in onto its shiny brass floor. The tube was large enough to accommodate two humans if they stood close together. He and Sera had used it at the same time and Marencourt could have fit in with him now, but it was a question of preference and personal space.

"See you there," the chief administrative elf said before Santa could ask if he wanted to ride together.

"Fenland forest," Santa said. The door of the tube closed and the cylinder dropped. It went down, past the ground floor and the cellar to connect into a base shaft. The conveyance then shifted to one of the tracks and sped onward until it halted and began to lift again. It reached the surface and the doors opened to the reindeer delegate headquarters. RDHQ was a rustic structure with impressive woodwork and large windows that revealed the forest beyond. Santa stepped out. RDHQ always had a scent of hay, pine and wood that was appealing to him.

"Santa," Fonteloi, an HHE, greeted. He had one of Santa's coats over his arm which he handed over. "The chief said you would need this."

"Yes. I should have thought about it." He put it on and they started for the door. "How are things?"

"Three have the infection so they are quarantined. Nerri is tending them. She has a particular affection for DJ."

Donner Junior had recently joined the team. "Are they in much discomfort?"

"It's not too bad," Fonteloi replied halfheartedly. "Or so they indicate. They are accepting the medication without argument. Usually, they are stubborn about it, but the fact that we're so close to the big event has them rattled. They want to be well enough to take part."

Santa understood. They stepped outside into the cold air and the crisp scents of snow and pine. Fenland was a lush forest of several thousand acres with marshes and bogs. There were five large stables, a training facility, a bunkhouse for reindeer hands, and a hall for dining and recreation. The reindeer trainers, there were four of them, and the reindeer delegates, there were six of them, had private housing for themselves and their families.

While a majority of city elves considered theirs to be an unenviable, secluded existence, those who resided and worked in Fenland Forest would have chosen no other life.

There were some three hundred head of reindeer in the North Pole herd and a few dozen hands that cared for them. Only the finest hands were promoted to the role of a delegate, and they were chosen by the reindeer themselves in a moving ceremony.

"Hot buttered rum?" Marencourt asked as he joined them with a floating tray that held three insulated mugs. He wore a thick overcoat with a colorful patchwork design that fell past his knees and he had donned furry boots.

"Thank you." Santa said as he accepted one.

"Fonteloi?" Marencourt offered.

"Thank you, chief, but I never imbibe on duty."

Marencourt shrugged. "Personally, I find while on duty to be the best time to drink."

The three walked on and the tray followed. As they topped a ridge, they saw a few dozen reindeer and an equal number of elves in the training field below observing ten reindeer that were paired up and in a line.

"In step, now," Julep Ajurian called from the middle of the field. Julep was the head trainer. "Walk."

The reindeer walked in perfect synchronization.

"Going into a trot in three, two, one, go!"

The reindeer trotted.

"Nice," Marencourt commented.

Fonteloi agreed. "There is a lot of talent to choose from."

"Next the side step," Julep called. "To the right. In three, two, one, go!"

The reindeer did a hoof over hoof side step.

"That one is difficult for them," Fonteloi said.

Santa was in awe. "Who knew they were so adroit?"

"Good," Julep praised the animals. "Face forward and stop." Julep raised a hand in greeting to Santa. "Hello, Santa," he called.

The other elves and the reindeer all turned to him. The elves bowed and waved. The reindeer bowed and then stood tall with pride. Santa lifted his hand in greeting and started toward them. Marencourt, Fonteloi and the tray followed, keeping a bit of distance behind.

Julep and his under-trainers came to greet them. The trainers and most of the hands were human height.

"Your Majesty," Julep said. "How good to see you."

"And you, Julep." He looked at the others. "Ewillam, Phonder, DeGrue."

"Hello, Santa," they greeted.

"We can imagine how busy you are," Julep said, "with the big day approaching. And we realize this was a blow. It was to all of us, most especially the afflicted, but we have fully capable reindeer to carry on. We train all year long, you know."

"Yes. I do know that. They look wonderful."

"Thank you. We're very proud of them. So, how would you like to proceed? Meet the reindeer first or see them perform?"

Santa noticed additional reindeer moving in from the stables and forest to watch the audition. The other hands and the families of the hands were hurrying closer as well. "I'd like to meet them. Are those ten on the field all prospects for the team?"

"Yes. We gave the flying team the afternoon off. They're having a shampoo, hoof manicure and massage."

"Ah."

The undertrainers hurried back to the reindeer on the field. Ewillam, the first to get there, gestured to the stag on the end beside him. "May I present Stanson," he called.

Stanson bowed.

"Gemini," DeGrue called next, referring to the second in line that he stood next to. Gemini bowed.

"Vix de Vixon," Phonder called referring to the third reindeer which then bowed.

Ewilliam had gone to the next deer in line, as did the other trainers until all the reindeer had been named. Thelphius, Hidolpho, Sigard, Deon, Defiant, Southstar and Maeter.

"I am glad to meet you all," Santa called.

Julep faced him. "As always with the flying team, the stags are very nearly the same height, sixty inches at their shoulder, and weight, five hundred and ten pounds. They all have very nearly the same leg length, antler height, eyesight and intelligence. Since the lineup is in order of seniority, the junior members will go in back."

Santa nodded.

"We'll get started then," Julep said. He started toward the field, but turned back to Santa. "I suggest an individual parade and then a show of teamwork. Shall we get the wings out?"

"I don't think that will be necessary unless you do."

Julep shook his head. "They are all flight tested and approved."

"All right, then," Santa said cheerfully.

"I imagine this will take a while," Marencourt added as Julep went to begin the audition.

"Yes," Santa agreed. "And I want to see the patients afterwards."

Marencourt sipped his drink. "May need more of these."

Chapter Nine
The Morning After

Santa was seated at the breakfast table waiting for Al the next morning when the partially open door blew wide open in typical, irate Marencourt fashion. The CAE entered with a livid expression. "You had the new Santa implanted with the knowledge of the ages?" he thundered.

"I thought he could handle it," Santa replied sheepishly.

Marencourt's fists were clenched tightly. "The last human to receive that much information was in the sixteenth century. A fellow by the name of Michel de Nostredame." When Santa did not appear to register recognition of the name, Marencourt huffed. "Also known as Nostradamus. Sound familiar?"

Santa's jaw went lax.

"He was no good to us after the knowledge implant. And *then* he went and blabbed about every catastrophe that would befall humans in the coming centuries! Surely you recall his name being mentioned in the selection committee meeting."

"No, I do not."

"Probably because Vestor was interrupting me at the time."

"Or vice versa," Santa retorted.

"Michel never got the opportunity to be Santa because his predecessor thought it would be easier to implant all the information in his brain rather than lead him through it. Lyudmil," he said bitterly. "He was called Lyudmil the ludicrous after that." Marencourt donned a ridiculous expression. "Michel is a smart man," he mocked in a thick foreign accent. "I thought he could handle it."

Santa realized he should have studied History of Santa better. "What happened to Michel?"

Marencourt's expression cleared and he shrugged. "He went back to his life, remarried, had six children and got famous from his writings of the future. So it wasn't all bad for him, I suppose. Naturally, his memory of being here was wiped from his mind but, sadly, nothing else. Somehow, the poor man saw centuries ahead of his time. Things he could not possibly comprehend."

"I didn't realize—"

"Then why not ask?" Marencourt rudely interrupted.

Santa rose. He was beginning to get angry himself. "If you recall, Marencourt, when you handed me the training curriculum, I said, 'so this is what he needs to know,' and you said yes, and then I asked, 'but not how he needs to learn it,' or something to that effect, and you said that was correct. Other than quickly." He paused before adding, "Time being of the essence," with an exaggerated bob of his head.

Marencourt scowled.

"So I got the information in his head quickly. Obviously, if I had realized that implanting the information might melt his mind and turn him into a raving lunatic or whatever it was that happened to Michel AKA Nostradamus, I would not have done it."

It was finally Marencourt's turn to look uncomfortable. "It's possible I may share a fraction of the blame," he muttered. This was followed by a prolonged sigh, because whatever damage had been done was well and truly done at this point. "I don't suppose you know where he is? Were you not supposed to meet at eight?"

Santa pulled out his pocket watch. It was twelve after the hour. "Perhaps he's sleeping late," he replied apprehensively.

Marencourt shook his head in disgust. "Yesterday, we had to select reindeer replacements. Today, it may be a new Santa."

Santa sat back down. His knees were suddenly weak. If he had damaged Al's mind, he would never forgive himself. Forget his own reign going down in flames and him being ranked as one of the worst Santas of all time, Al deserved to be Santa. The man was meant to be Santa. Why had he ordered the implantation? Laziness! That was why. It was inexcusable.

"Where is Al Dorsett?" Marencourt asked.

Santa looked at him in puzzlement but then realized he was asking his assistants.

"I saw him running, Chief," was the response. "He looked feverish."

Santa squeezed his eyes shut. His failure was crushing the breath from him.

"He is not in his room," another voice said.

"Not on the grounds," another voice said.

"Not in the hospital ward."

"Not in the chapel."

Santa couldn't breathe. He felt ill.

"I am so sorry I'm late," Al said, bursting into the room and causing Santa and Marencourt to jump. "I'm starved and I imagine you are, too. Hello, Marencourt. I hope you're well." As Al went to his place, filled bowls and platters began to appear on the table. "*Mmm*. Poached Eggs. And fresh scones. They smell heavenly. Oh and the fruit is gorgeous."

Santa looked at Marencourt who looked back at him with no less astonishment.

Al was eagerly filling his plate oblivious to their bewilderment. "I went for a ralk around the manor this morning," he said cheerfully. "It was so invigorating."

"A ralk?" Santa repeated, trying to sound normal. His legs did not feel capable of lifting or supporting him so getting a plate of breakfast was out of the question.

"Well, I am not a runner, per se, but I run in short bursts and then I walk until I can run again. Ralking. It's a cross between running and walking. An amusing lady I know made the term up and said I could borrow it. She said the sport wasn't pretty but it was effective and usually the best us old folk can do." He barked a laugh and then eagerly tucked into the meal.

Marencourt came forward. Reaching the table, he asked Santa if he would care for a plate. It was as close to an apology as Marencourt would get, although Santa did not feel he deserved an apology anyway. He felt as if he had been granted a nearly miraculous reprieve, one that only he and Marencourt would ever know about. "Yes, please."

Marencourt waved his hand and food came to a plate, which came to his hand. He handed it over. "Thank you," Santa said.

Marencourt nodded and then looked quizzically at Al. "I understand you had Santa knowledge implanted."

Al nodded. When he finished his bite and wiped his lips, he said, "Indeed, I did. I do believe I see the world all differently now. It is filled with even more wonder than I'd guessed." He went back to eating.

Santa managed a bite of cream cheese Danish as Ree appeared with a steaming cup of coffee and a look of understanding. "I put something special in it," she said under her breath. Curious, he took a sip. It tasted the same as usual, two sugars and cream, but then he got a soothing, contented feeling. *All is well,* seemed to whisper in his brain. "Thank you, Ree."

She smiled and retreated.

"Yesterday, after the virtual tour," Al said, "I felt a debilitating fatigue come over me. Vestor assured me it was normal for having traveled between realms, so I asked to ski then."

Santa and Marencourt looked baffled. "Ski?" Santa asked.

"Oh, sorry. Have the Santa knowledge implant then."

"SKI," Santa repeated. Santa Knowledge Implant. "And what was it like?" he asked warily.

Al looked at a loss. "I'm not sure how to describe it. It was like having everything about myself opened wider. My mind, my spirit, my heart. Everything opened in yearning and was filled with knowledge. I don't remember all of it or falling asleep."

Marencourt grunted and nodded. "It will come to you as you need it."

"Yes! I *do* keep thinking things I did not know before. I even checked the shape of my head this morning to make sure it hadn't swelled from all the information, but … it was still as handsome as ever." He threw back and laughed a hearty "ho-ho-ho." Then he gasped in surprise by the sound. "I have your laugh!"

"Actually," Santa said, "I don't think I ever did it that well."

"No, you didn't," Marencourt concurred.

"I cannot wait to see the annexes for myself," Al gushed. "All that technology! Are we doing that next?"

"Yes," Santa replied. "We can."

"I also can't wait to see the city with my own eyes. Then there are the children's letters we should go through and make sure everything is order. I will assist you however you need. And there's the business of my contract to take care of. I am ready to sign." He went back to eating and Santa and Marencourt exchanged another look. "And the reindeer," Al added. "I am so anxious to meet them all. How are they?" he asked with concern.

Santa nodded and started to reply but Al, satisfied it was an affirmative, continued.

"Let's see. There's Kasick and Fabian and Maximus and Fulsome," he began. "I wonder if I can put it to music," he mused.

"Let's not," Marencourt said, accepting a cup of chai tea from a floating tray.

Al chuckled. "Who were the three selected?"

"Thelphius, Deon and Gemini," Santa replied.

"Ah." Al leaned back in his chair, satiated. "Regarding what I learned, I must say, I cannot help being a fan of Saint Nicholas. I know he's not the favorite of some elves but we owe so much of our identity to him."

Marencourt grunted in disapproval. "The legend did not come about with Nicholas. It has been in existence since before your recorded history. Even *in* your recorded history, there was Odin in the fourth century who, by the way, looked a great deal like the two of you. He rode an-eight legged flying horse named Sleipnir."

"A flying horse," Al said thoughtfully.

Marencourt nodded. A chair was suddenly there which he sat in. "Nicholas of Bari helped further the legend, but he was what is commonly referred to as high maintenance. He didn't come up with a single new addition to our repertoire. He was too busy battling the persecution of Christians. Which was noble," he conceded. "Persecution of any sort is ugly, but he had responsibility with us. Instead, we'd find him in a prison cell having been arrested again and have to transport him back here."

"He was a man of great passion," Santa mused.

Al nodded. "And conviction."

"Agreed," Marencourt admitted. "And he was popular. The word Sinterklaas means Saint Nicholas. So there's that. In the middle ages, Sinterklaas put money in the boots of poor people. Sound suggestive of any tradition that you know of?"

"Of course," Al said, enjoying the discourse. "First the idea of giving to those in need and then putting gifts in stockings."

Marencourt nodded. "But the overall legend of Santa came about bit by bit, occasionally inspired by rascally elves. That's one of the reasons DCV's were banned."

"DCV's," Al murmured. "Meaning direct contact visit. Elf to human."

"Correct. They are banned except for top-level authority. Meaning—" Marencourt gestured between the men.

Santa chuckled. "I believe Marencourt is referring to the writing of a certain poem. *A visit from St. Nicholas."*

Al smiled. "Twas the night before Christmas."

"Indeed," Marencourt said dryly. "Who could have guessed the success of the thing? It was published anonymously in eighteen-twenty-three, but two years before that there was a booklet called *A New Year's Present to the Little Ones from Five to Twelve,* also by an anonymous author, that went, *Old Santeclaus with much delight, His reindeer drives this frosty night. O'er chimneytops, and tracks of snow, To bring his yearly gifts to you.* "

Santa looked thoughtful. "It's not as catchy, is it?"

Al leaned forward and peered at Marencourt. "Who actually wrote Twas the Night Before Christmas?" he asked excitedly. "Clement Clarke Moore or Henry Livingston? It's still hotly debated."

Marencourt waved off the question. "Livingston or Moore, Moore or Livingston? Does it really matter? I assure you, it does not to those gentlemen. I can tell you the elf responsible for leaking the information used in the poem. Beldernaut Flibberstich. He was scolded, demoted and publicly shamed, and then we had the policy change on DCV's. Beldernaut revealed the names of some of our finest reindeer, which they did not appreciate. Reindeer do not desire fame."

Al was intrigued. "So Beldernaut appeared to …the real author, whoever he was, and—"

"They had drinks and laughs," Marencourt replied, "smoked pipes, a bit of opium—"

Al's jaw dropped.

"It was not illegal," Marencourt said defensively. "It wasn't even that uncommon."

"It is a good poem," Santa said to Marencourt who shrugged with indifference.

"And influential," Al said.

"True," Marencourt allowed, "But before that, in 1809, I believe, a fellow named Knickerbocker, who was actually the author Washington Irving, wrote *A History of New York*, also almost certainly inspired by an elf, although which elf was not discovered. The point is, several things were established in that work and then merely repeated in the *influential* poem."

"Such as?" Al asked.

"Santa riding over the tops of the trees bringing yearly gifts to children," Marencourt said. "Santa smoking his pipe and the smoke rising over and around his head. Oh! Laying a finger aside of his nose, he rises and flies away again in his wagon."

Al nodded in appreciation. "Interesting."

"The human in Knickerbocker's fable was Oloffe who realizes Santa has come from a far-off place, a kingdom with palaces and domes and spires." Marencourt shook his head. "Had the elf that shared that information been caught, he or she might well have faced charges of treason. It's far too close to the truth. You haven't seen our city yet, but you will see."

"I cannot wait," Al said breathlessly.

"Yes," Santa said quietly, almost a sigh. He was strangely tired from the excitement of the morning.

Al eyed a delectable looking creampuff. "Oh maybe just one more," he said reaching for it.

"Don't be proud," Marencourt urged Santa quietly. "Use a glide disc for the tour."

Santa nodded. Maybe he would.

<u>Chapter Ten</u>
Annex A

"It's a glide disc," Marencourt explained to Al as Santa stepped on a clear round disc. It began to glimmer and then it rose ever so slightly. Marencourt and Al started walking and Santa glided along with them.

"But how does it work?" Al asked.

"See the blades of the fans turning?" Marencourt asked.

Al studied it with a cocked head as he walked. The blades were also clear, but with tiny silver strands. That's what caused the glimmering effect.

"Each of the fans can rotate up to a million times a minute."

"So the force of the fans—" Al puzzled.

"It's a complex device," Marencourt interrupted. "But, yes, the force of the air from the fans keeps the thing up. There are also electromagnets and a superconductor and a stabilizing unit."

"How does it know where to go?"

"The rider controls it. It takes a bit of practice, but you use the pressure of your feet to direct it."

Santa was content to let Marencourt do the explaining. Explanations took so much effort.

"Annex A is through here," the elf said as he opened a panel at the end of the corridor with a wave of his hand. Beyond it was a long walkway with a dome of opaque glass over it. At the far end was a door of smoky glass that continually changed colors.

Marencourt led the way through it and into a massive room with hundreds of elves seated or standing in individual workstations. The focus of each elf was on an orb in front of them that showed a child at work or play. There were no sounds from the mini-movies. The only sounds in the room were elves talking to one another or recording their findings.

"This is Olo. Observation, level one," Santa said.

Al nodded. "A general looksee at how a child is doing."

"Correct. If a problem is noted, say unusual behavior, being destructive or mean-spirited, the file is kicked up to level two."

"If the elves of level two are concerned," Marencourt interjected, "the case goes to Investigations."

Al went closer to a workstation drawing the attention of the elf within. "Do you want in?" the elf offered.

"I would, thank you."

The elf got up and moved and Al sat in front of the three dimensional digital display.

"You can use the wireless earpiece or just bring the screen in," the elf explained. "Like so," the elf said, waving the display forward until Al was encapsulated in it. Al drew in a sharp breath of wonder as he watched a girl of eight or nine talking to a group of other girls, holding court, as it were.

Santa watched. He knew the child. She was popular and had very involved parents. Her character was still in flux, but she was too often inclined toward mean-girl behavior.

"You know," Marencourt said to Santa, "you could excuse yourself."

Santa looked at him.

"Your protégé will want to visit every division and see, if not try out, every piece of technology in the facility. We'll be hours."

It was true and even the thought of it was tiring. But wasn't it his responsibility?

"I can show him," Marencourt offered. "You could go back to the office and look over the addendum to the contract he needs to be made aware of."

"An addendum? What addendum?"

"It's better if you read it, since you'll be explaining it to him when we finish here."

Santa did not like being left out of things, but he was too tired to argue.

Al rejoined them. "It was as if I was there," he marveled. "I believe she needs to go to level two," he added.

Santa agreed. "The problem is she gets everything she wants."

"Lucky her," Al said.

"I'm not of that opinion," Santa rejoined. "But you'll make up your own mind."

"Santa is going to his office to work for a bit," Marencourt said. "I will show you around here."

"Level two Observation?" Al asked.

"Yes. And Investigations and news gathering and file keeping. Also gift intelligence is on this floor. Then, in the mezzanine, we have a cafeteria—"

"The best grilled cheese sandwich and tomato soup you have ever tasted," Santa interjected.

"As well as BOA," Marencourt said, "the bureau of ordering and arrangements, and internal logistics and facilitation. Then on the top floor, is flight logistics and satellite management. They plan the route every year. It's a very impressive operation. Coordinating flight paths while avoiding international conflicts and no-fly zones and military surveillance."

Al was riveted, and Santa was realizing what a good idea it was for him to escape.

"Shall we?" Marencourt asked Al, gesturing onward.

"Yes!"

"I'll see you afterwards," Santa said, already gliding on. A long dormant phrase from his youth, 'get while the gettin' is good' occurred to him, making him chuckle to himself.

Two hours later, Santa had napped, had lunch and read the addendum. He was thinking about how to share it with Al when Marencourt's voice was heard.

"Santa?"

Santa slid his reading glasses off. "Yes?"

Marencourt appeared as a hologram. "We will be a while longer," he said with obvious displeasure. "Your successor is a never-ending fount of questions."

Santa restrained a smile. "That is how one learns," he said complacently.

"Isn't it easy to be smug when you are there and I am here? Anyway, it will be another few hours before he rejoins you."

"Understood." Marencourt vanished and Santa chuckled. He rose, stretched and then made his way to the viewing room to catch up on some of his cases. He sat and was about to order an update when he had another thought. "Another seat, please." A seat appeared beside his. "A hologram of Sera." A hologram of Sera formed in the seat. She smiled at him. "Hello, my dear," he said softly.

"Hello," she returned. Her voice had an airy, recorded quality, but it was her voice.

He reluctantly turned back to the screen. "The DCV footage with Charles Fuller, please."

The room darkened and, on the screen, was a brick house as the front door was approached. A small fist knocked low on the door.

"Let me ring," said a spiffily dressed male elf. He made a tugging motion and a deep bell gonged in the home. "What?" he asked his companion as if he'd gotten a sour look. Apparently the recording device was on the companion.

The front door opened to reveal a wary looking man of seventy five. Charles Fuller. He looked very tall, but only because the elves were standard-height.

"Mr. Fuller," said a female elf who wore the recording device. "I believe you were expecting us."

He didn't speak for a moment. "I don't know what I was expecting," he uttered. He glanced out to the street. "Can other people see you?"

"Not with your overgrown shrubbery," she replied.

His brow quirked at the snarky response, but he stepped back to allow them in.

They entered a spacious, but dated, living room. "May we sit?" the female elf asked.

"Yes. Please." Mr. Fuller led the way and sat.

The camera rose as the elf gracefully took a seat. Given the smoothness, she probably had mini glide discs attached to her shoes. Her companion chose a round ottoman and then discovered it swiveled. He whirled himself around for the fun of it. Noticing the she-elf's less than thrilled gaze, he said, "What?"

"*Gar-some dignitui*," she replied scornfully.

Have. Some. Dignity. The words occurred to Santa as clearly as if they had been spoken.

"What's this about then?" the old man asked.

"That has been explained in some detail, Mr. Fuller," she replied calmly.

"In a dream, by an elf," he retorted.

"Three nights in a row," she said patiently. "And, as requested, after the third visitation, you wrote down the names of the Follett family in your notebook and put it in your desk drawer."

He frowned. "How do you know that?"

"Are you willing?" she asked. "That is the only question. It is time to act."

He huffed. "What would I say? Besides, it doesn't seem proper. An old man, a pretty younger woman, little girls."

"It is more than proper. It is right. Are you willing? It is the only question."

He folded his arms stubbornly. "It doesn't seem like the only question to me."

"You have no nefarious thoughts about them or about anything else."

"Of course, I don't! That's not the point. What would people think?"

"What people?"

"Just show him," the male elf urged. "Here. I will." He pulled out a pocket watch looking device and flipped it open. He turned it so the curious man could see. A beam of light was projected outward from it showing the scene that had transpired between Beth

Follett and her landlord followed by her children's reaction.

"That was a rotten thing to do," Charles muttered when he'd watched. "With all this virus business going on. He oughtn't to have done that. It was wrong."

"Yes," the she-elf agreed.

The he-elf clicked the top of the device and the scene changed. Now Samantha labored over a letter to Santa. Dear Santa was written in uneven letters, mostly capital letters. "We need a house," she murmured aloud as she wrote the words, although she wrote *ned* for need and *hows* for house.

Charles Fuller's expression softened as he watched the girl and her younger sister next to her. The younger one's hands were on the table, her face pressed against them. "Can Santa get us a house?" she asked worriedly.

Samantha looked at her. "I don't know," she admitted. But she looked like she did know and the answer was not a good one.

"They have lived in their automobile," the she-elf said. "Currently, they are in a shelter."

"With limited time left," the he-elf added.

Mr. Fuller sighed. "Suppose I wouldn't mind meeting them, but—"

"Excellent," the female elf interrupted. The camera moved as she got down from her seat. "The address of the shelter is written below their names in your notebook, which is next to a token of our esteem. Good day." She turned for the door.

"Wait a minute," Charles said.

She turned back. "Yes?"

He seemed stumped. "I don't know. I've never had a visit from an elf before, much less two of them."

"Then we are even, good sir. We have never visited a Charles F. Fuller before. It was most satisfactory. Santa will be pleased. Ta-ta."

Santa chuckled and looked over at his wife's hologram smiling back at him. "Next," Santa called.

Seventeen-year-old Tommy Leonard was seated at the kitchen table finishing a quiz. Next to him sat Catherine Johnson, a middle-aged tutor from the same apartment building. She had ash-blonde hair streaked with silver strands. Next to Catherine sat Liam coloring a hand-drawn map of some sort.

Liam looked up at Catherine who grinned and nodded at his work. He smiled and went back to it. Catherine looked at her watch. "Time," she said to Tommy.

He sighed and then smiled. "Okay." He pushed the paper toward her and she began grading it.

The boys' dad, Curt, walked into the room wearing jeans and a sweatshirt. It was a Saturday, Santa realized. "What smells so good?" Curt asked.

"Catherine made meatloaf," Tommy replied.

Curt peeked in the pans atop the stove. "And mashed potatoes and green beans." He took an appreciate whiff. "If I could bottle that smell, I'd spray it every day."

Tommy gave him a look. "I kind of get it, but how disappointing would it be when we only had tuna casserole for dinner?"

"Good point," his dad conceded. "Not that your tuna casserole isn't killer."

Tommy laughed. "Yeah, right."

Liam looked at Catherine. "Can I face-time Kalee now?"

Catherine looked at his paper and then at him. "If it's okay with your dad."

"Sure," Curt said.

Catherine pulled her phone from her pocket and handed it over and Liam took it and left the kitchen. Kalee was Catherine's granddaughter and she Liam had become face-time buddies. How wonderful that one lady had made a difference in the lives of Curt Easton's family. She'd become an honorary grandmother, and they had enriched her life, as well.

"Excellent," Catherine said to Tommy when the grading was complete. "But be careful with the 'select all the right answer' questions. You missed this one," she said, pointing one out.

"Tommy will do well," Santa murmured. "They all will. Next."

Lakeisha Crenshaw was outside The Children's Home, throwing a tennis ball against the building and catching it on an overcast winter day. A slightly older girl hurried toward her, saying, "There you are."

Keisha threw and caught the ball again.

"They finished setting up the Christmas shop," the other girl said excitedly. "The little kids get to go first, but there's some cool stuff."

Keisha gave her a droll look.

"What?" the other girl asked. "Come on. You get to pick out something for anybody you want. And they have a Christmas wrapping station set up, too. So you can wrap it, too."

Keisha rolled her eyes and kept throwing. "Same as every year."

"So?"

"So. Boring."

The girl huffed. "It is not."

Keisha turned to her with a wry expression. "We get to pick out a five-dollar present for somebody else and wrap it. *Whoo-hoo*. And then the Churchy-church do-gooders will leave us all a package to unwrap on Christmas morning. Let's see? What will be in it? Underwear and socks and a shirt and, *ooh*, something fun," she mocked. "Last year I got a jewelry kit. Isn't that cool?"

"You liked that kit."

Lakeisha turned and threw the ball again.

"Besides," the girl (her name was Darcy) said. "This is different. You get to pick something out for someone else."

Lakeisha shrugged. "I don't feel like it."

Darcy was miffed. She whirled around and started to stomp off, but she turned back for a parting shot. "You're selfish, Keisha. That's what you are."

Keisha caught the ball and then looked after her friend who was walking away. She scowled at the wall, as if it were to blame, and then threw the ball with all her might. She missed catching it for the first time and then turned to go after it with a frown and tears shining in her eyes.

Santa sighed. "How to reach her," he said under his breath. "How do we reach her?"

Chapter Eleven
Contracts and Clauses

Al was still buoyed by the tour of Annex A when he met Santa in the office. "I have been over the contract word for word," he declared cheerily. "I am ready to sign. In fact, I'm trembling with excitement to sign."

"Yes," Santa said reluctantly. "I can see that. Well—"

Al's face clouded over with worry. "Is something wrong?"

"No," Santa assured him. "Not at all. It's just that an addendum is being offered."

"An addendum?"

Santa nodded slowly, wondering how to phrase it. "A provision allowing for ... well, for a wife."

Al blinked. "Excuse me?"

Santa passed the contract over turned to page 104. "Your ... Mrs. Claus, CJ—"

Al's eyes were as round as saucers. "What about her?" he asked breathlessly.

"She can join you. If you wish. As your wife."

"My wife? B-become my wife?"

"Yes. She was approached, the same as the other candidates, the same as you were. And she's willing. Actually, more than willing. She is anxious to assume the role."

Al bolted out of his chair. "CJ! Become my wife?"

Santa nodded warily. He wasn't certain if Al was about to burst into song or tears. Or both. The man was trembling.

"Yes!" Al cried. "Oh, yes! Oh, thank you! Yes!"

A few moments of silence lapsed. "You'd like to think about it then?" Santa asked with a straight face. Then he grinned.

Al laughed his now signature ho-ho-ho as he sat back down. His cheeks were red, his eyes gleaming. Santa could not help but be reminded of lines from the celebrated poem. *His eyes, how they twinkled, his dimples, how merry, his cheeks were like roses, his nose like a cherry.* If fact, darned if he didn't have a sudden craving for his pipe.

"CJ," Al marveled. "Oh, Santa. I've been in love with her for ever so long."

"I am glad for you, my friend. It is so beneficial and so much more fulfilling to have a helpmate. I only wish you could have known my Sera."

"So do I. But I will know her, won't I? Say in fifty-eight years or so."

Santa smiled and nodded.

Al scribbled his signature at the bottom of the contract. "When will CJ arrive?"

"On Christmas Day," Santa replied. He reached for his pipe. "How is that for a Christmas gift? Oh," he said recalling something. He set the pipe aside. "There is one other decision to be made."

"What's that?"

"Age."

"Age?" Al repeated.

"You're not the typical Santa-designate. Usually, they are between thirty-five and forty-five years of age."

"Right," Al said softly.

"On the first Christmas each new Santa is here, they, I should say we, wake to find ourselves feeling younger. Looking younger. We are, indeed, younger by a few years. It is quite a high. It's the same for our spouses. Then, over the next fifty-eight years, we proceed to age at half the normal rate. So we generally end up anywhere from sixty-five to seventy years of age by the end of our term. I am closer to seventy at this point, or maybe even beyond it, but it has been a difficult year."

"I know it has," Al sympathized.

"The point is that you can choose to turn back the hands of time. You and CJ. At the end of your term, you will not be a great deal older than you are now."

"Wha—what's the decision to be made?"

"If you prefer, you can stay the age you are. You're healthy and fit. Should you choose that option, you will age very little for the next fifty-eight years."

"Uh, no. I would not choose that option. I would choose youth. Youth. Yes, definitely youth. To be thirty-five again? Oh, yes. I would choose that."

"So you'd like to think about it?" Santa teased.

Al burst into laughter, but then he sobered. "You don't think CJ would choose differently, do you?"

Santa shook his head. "I've not yet known the lady who would."

"Oh, my. This will be a special Christmas!"

Chapter Twelve
An Pole Othrond

S anta watched Al for his reaction since it was
the first time he had stepped outside the
manor. He'd been transported from earth to
Annex B and crossed through the enclosed walkway to
the manor, and that is where they had been since,
getting him up to speed. Today was to be a quick tour
of the city and thus Al's first walk in the great
outdoors.

Al, wearing a snappy blue overcoat, cashmere scarf
and fedora, stopped and blinked. "Of course," he
exclaimed. "Here I've been thinking frigid North Pole,
but we're in a different realm."

Santa nodded. "Yes, we are. Located above the
Earth's North Pole." He pointed to the sky. "Our sun,
is—"

"I know this," Al said excitedly, just realizing it.
"Polaris!"

"Polaris B," Vestor said having just joined them
wearing a plum colored coat and beanie that was
particularly striking with his lavender eyes. "Hello!"

"Good morning, Vestor," Santa greeted. "Now, we
could get to the Nipst station faster," Santa explained
to Al, "but I thought you'd enjoy a walk in the fresh air
and sunshine." The sparkling snow was rapidly
melting because it was sunny and probably forty
degrees.

"You're right. I would," Al replied. He turned to face the mansion behind him and admire the view with his own eyes. He looked at Santa with a curious expression. "It's funny how I know things, but I don't know that I know them until … I know them. Does that make sense?"

Santa nodded. He was grateful that knowledge implantation had improved since the sixteenth century. "Shall we?" He strode forward as did the others. He had worn his favorite overcoat, a plaid muffler and a jaunty cap. "What a perfectly lovely day."

"It really is," Vestor agreed exuberantly.

"There are four seasons here," Al murmured.

"Yes," Santa replied. "Although summer is mild and lasts only a matter of weeks."

"Spring begins in April," Al said, realizing it as he said it.

"Late April," Vestor supplied. "Sometimes May."

"And winter begins in early November."

"It's been mild this year," Santa commented. "Oh, but the big snows are coming. In a month's time, we'll have three or four feet on the ground." Or rather *they* would have three feet on the ground. He would be elsewhere with Sera.

"The summer sanctuary," Al said curiously. "I don't seem to know much about that."

"That's because you'll craft it," Santa replied. "Each Claus gets to choose what goes into it and how warm it is. It's the most wonderful diversion when you're craving hot sun and a swim and trees in full leaf. Strawberries and lush green grass. In January, our weather can be freezing with a bitter wind and several feet of snow on the ground. But you step through the gates of the sanctuary and—" He smiled wistfully.

"Instantly, it is tropical. I'll take you and CJ to ours after Christmas."

Al radiated happiness. "I sometimes feel this is a dream."

Santa understood the feeling well. "It is often a dream. Try and remember that when the work piles up and complications arise and compound. When you feel you're not good enough for the job and you can't possibly do it all. When all you can see is how much you can't get done, rather than the good you are doing." He saw that Al looked solemn. "We love all children and we serve them, but we can't reach them all every year. We do what we can, all of us, but we always want to do more."

Al stopped short and blinked. "Are there really one billion, nine hundred million children on earth right now?"

"Yes. And so many of them are in need. Some in need of things, food, clothing, shoes. Some in need of love and understanding. Or just hope. I promise you the pressure of the job will get to you from time to time. Just know that it's natural. And then go take a break. Have a picnic in the summer sanctuary with your wife. Talk with her. Tell what you're feeling. Don't try to hold it all inside and handle everything yourself."

Al nodded.

They walked on in silence until they passed through the grand gates of the manor. Across a street was parkland. "See the gazebo there?" Santa asked pointing it out.

"Yes."

"It's one of many. Obviously, they can be used for sitting and resting or waiting out a rain shower in the spring, but they also provide entryways to the underpass."

"Which is similar to a subway," Al said.

"Yes, but in a small car," Santa replied. "Big enough for one or two of us. More elves can fit in, of course. We'll take it to the nipst station." He grinned. "And get this show on the road."

The North Pole Sky Tram had three cars, each with two seats facing two seats with a table in between. Al sat facing forward, Santa sat next to him and Vestor sat across from Santa.

As the tram started in motion, Al put on the available earphones and peered out the window with the excitement of a child taking in a magical theme park for the first time. He listened a moment before he got a surprised look on his face. He pulled off the ear phones and held them closer for Santa to hear. Vestor also leaned closer to hear.

'An Pole Othrond na- a metropolis an I galadrim i bui- i tradition –o mel, service a giving an all núr sui exemplified bui Santa Claus.'

"Elvish," Santa explained.

"Of course," Al said. He stuck it away. "I don't need them anyway when I have the best tour guides in the world. But what was it saying?"

"North Pole City is a metropolis for elves that uphold the tradition of love, service and giving for all people as exemplified by Santa Claus," Vestor replied.

"How lovely," Al said softly. He looked out the window. "*An Pole Othrond.* It's so much bigger than I expected."

"Had you pictured a quaint village?" Santa asked.

Al shrugged and then nodded. He looked at Vestor. "I hope that's not insulting."

"Not at all," Vestor rejoined. "There are quaint villages. Hundreds of them."

"Down there is the toy district," Santa pointed out. "It goes ten blocks this way and twenty blocks deep. We acquire a good deal from earth's manufacturers, of course, but they still make the most marvelous toys right down there."

"I can't wait to see all of it! Walk through every shop and store."

The tram traversed onward and Al was awestruck. Many of the brick streets below had been swept clear of snow. Charmingly shaped trees and shrubbery were lit with lights. There were pretty lampposts and benches, and the colorful shops, (so many shops!) had fanciful architecture. Some were tall, others so small that it was hard to believe they could accommodate HHE's. There were clothing shops, candy shops, sporting goods shops, shoe shops, bookstores and furniture stores. There were hotels. A spa. Hair stylists. A clockmakers shop had a large, intricate cuckoo clock on the top of the building. A hat store had a hat floating above it.

"The hat changes every day," Vestor said.

"And here is the food district," Santa said. There were restaurants of every cuisine and taverns and pubs and bistros and tea shops and bakeries and coffee shops. Intoxicating scents drifted upward to them.

"My mouth is watering," Al remarked.

"We'll have lunch after this," Santa said.

"What is that small castle?"

"That's our museum," Vestor replied. "Elfkind through the ages. We call it The Castle."

"The crystal turret in front," Santa said, "that's where we watch the parade."

"Ah."

Elf Cathedral, on the other side of the tram, was breathtaking. There was nothing fanciful about it. On either side of the cathedral were parks, and to the side and rear of the parks were schools, elfkin-minder communities and libraries.

"It's brilliant," Al marveled. "Just brilliant."

The tram had reached the highest point and was gradually starting down. They passed a picturesque residential area and an ice-skating rink and a Ferris wheel.

"When we reach the next station," Santa said. "It's a bit of a wild ride to the connecting station."

"I love it," Vestor blurted. "I always giggle. I can't help it."

Al looked at Santa. "And you?"

Santa drew back with a half-hearted frown. "Santa does not giggle. Santa laughs from the belly!"

"Of course," Al played along. "Now if I remember correctly, Nipst is, in essence, a triangle."

"Correct," Vestor said.

"So we began at Station A," Al continued, "and went up and now down. It was fabulous. I couldn't even say my favorite part."

"Personally," Santa said, "I enjoy restaurant row, especially the pubs. And the doll shop. Wait until you see the doll shop."

Vestor was nodding. "And there is a shop for snow globes that is beyond belief. They have a life-size sphere you can go into and it is just like being inside a snow globe. You're lifted and suspended in weightlessness."

"Ingenious," Al replied. "So then Station B shoots us to Station C which leads us up and then down ending back at A."

"You've got it," Santa said.

"And on the C line," Al said, trying to recall his map.

"The C line goes higher than the A line," Vestor said. "So you'll see farms and ranches beyond the city. And plenty of quaint villages. You'll see the warehouse district, which is very large, and City Hall and Symphony Hall, which are both exquisite, and the post office and the bank."

"There won't be time for us to go through the shops before Christmas," Santa said. "And everything shuts down the week after."

"Everything?"

"Well, not some of the pubs, of course. They do a bang-up business. And restaurants. Any business can stay open if they chose to, but it's customary to close and rest the week after Christmas."

Al grunted. "Makes sense. And we'll have ample time after that." Al smiled, and Santa knew he was thinking about discovering the joys of the city with CJ on his arm just as he and Sera had done countless times.

They reached the bottom of the line and the car rounded a bend into a tunnel. It rocked, jostled and nearly stopped. Santa's breath caught because he knew what came next. Vestor giggled and they had not even moved yet. And then they did, accelerating to more than eighty miles per hour in nanoseconds. The bottom of Santa's stomach lurched and he squealed and laughed with delight. Anyone else might have called it a giggle.

~~~

That night, Santa couldn't sleep for an odd restlessness, a worry that he had not kept up with something. He knew he had slipped both physically and mentally these last months. Thank Heaven a worthy new Santa was on the brink of his new reign.

It had been a good day. Santa's only regret was Sera not being there to share it with. The longing for her never let up. He could get distracted for a time but, once he was not, the ache of loneliness returned. Now he wandered the corridors with his hands shoved in the pockets of a well-worn robe and slippers. Underneath the robe, he wore comfortable pajamas.

He paused in front of the library doors and then went inside. The room had stocked twenty-foot mahogany bookshelves and couches and tables. At present, the only occupants of the large room were ghostly swaths of moonlight from the long windows that seemed eerily alive.

In the back of the library were alcoves and smaller rooms. One of them was Sera's nook. It had been her place to read and relax and think. He made his way there. Reaching it caused an immediate pang of sorrow but, after a few deep breaths, it subsided enough to recognize a bittersweet pleasure. She had loved this spot and for good reason. The ceiling was lower here and the far end of the alcove was rounded and featured a bowed window with beveled glass panels. Reflected moonlight caused them to glow.

He went to her chaise lounge and stretched out on it. Beside it was a table with a tiffany lamp and a half-inch thick oval glass slab held in place by brass and copper hardware and attached to a base of brass and copper legs. It was a strange looking and yet pretty thing, but it had a purpose. When the glass was flicked firmly, it spun and created an image that rose and came to life in front of you. Sera had discovered its usefulness in helping to clear her mind or put a worry to rest. If she had been dwelling on a recollection, the memory would play out as clearly as when it occurred. If she had been wondering where he was or worried he was working too hard, she would see him.

What was it he wanted to see? What was nagging at him, feeling undone? He flicked the glass and watched it spin. What appeared was an image of a lady with strawberry blonde hair, wearing a face mask. Beth Follett. She had just been shown in to Mr. Fuller's home. Both of them looked uncomfortable as he invited her to sit. She sat with her hands in her lap. She had not yet taken off her coat or removed the purse strap from her shoulder.

"Feel free to take off the mask," he said.

She hesitated and then removed it.

"You didn't bring the children then?" Mr. Fuller asked.

Beth looked startled. "How do you know about my children?"

"I was told about them," he stammered. "The same as I was told about you."

"By whom?" she asked softly. "Not that I'm not grateful for the offer," she added quickly. "I am. But I don't understand."

105

"It's a live-in housekeeper position," he replied mildly. "What is there to understand?"

"Why me?"

He took a few moments to begin. "A well-meaning ... person found out about your situation and wanted to see you helped. This person also realized I could use some help. So, they got word to me to contact you." He took a breath and exhaled forcefully. "That was unbelievably difficult."

She barked a small laugh. "So the position entails taking care of the house."

"And cooking. And shopping."

She nodded. "I can do all of that."

"I can still drive myself here and there, but I have terrible night vision. Not that I need to go out much at night."

"And you don't mind the thought of two little girls living here?"

"I don't mind at all or I wouldn't have offered."

"They are good girls but they argue sometimes."

"Of course, they do. They're children." He smiled. "Shall I show you around the house?"

"The girls are with me," she admitted. "A friend drove us and I asked them to wait in the car."

He nodded slowly. "I understand. Do I pass the inspection?"

She looked apologetic.

"As much I can at this point," he added. "And don't feel badly for that. With two little ones, anyone would do the same."

Tears filled her eyes and she nodded rapidly. "I do want the job. And I thank you for offering it. It feels like a life saver."

"I think we will all enrich one another's life," he said. He stood and she did the same. He offered his hand and she reached out and shook it. "Now," he said, "I'll go put on some tea. And find some juice and cookies for the girls. If you want to bring them in, that is."

"I do. Thank you, Mr. Fuller."

"It's Frank," he said. "Charles Franklin, but my friends always called me Frank. And may I call you Beth?"

"Yes. Please do," she said with a smile.

Santa sighed. Beth Follett and her girls probably represented his biggest challenge of the year. That's what had been worrying him, but his think tank had done well on the Fuller-Follett arrangement. He felt it in his bones.

BOOK III: THE BIG EVENTS

Chapter Fourteen
The Inaugural Ride

S anta hummed *Deck the Halls* as he combed his beard and mustache. He'd soaked in a relaxing bubble bath that smelled of berries, raspberries if he wasn't mistaken, plus a bit of vanilla and sandalwood. He'd enjoyed a glass of champagne, (or had it been two?) and sung his favorite carols boisterously. He'd always thought he sang *I Saw Three Ships* particularly well.

This was his final Christmas Eve which was a cause for celebration in so many ways. Not only was Christmas Eve his night to shine, but they were nearing the end of a difficult year and there was every reason to believe next year would be better. God willing, the Covid-19 pandemic would finally be halted.

Santa pulled his suspenders over the shoulders of his white mock turtleneck and leaned over to admire the gleam of his dress boots under his red wool pants. All he had left to do was pull on his coat, gloves and hat, but he wouldn't do that until the last minute.

Normally, at this time, he would be chatting with Sera as they readied themselves for the parade. She would be in a red dress and look beautiful in it. His suit never changed a great deal, but she'd worn something new every year. In seventeen days, he would see her again. Yet another reason for celebration.

At three o'clock in the afternoon, he knocked on Al's door. Al opened it wearing white pants, dress boots, and a white turtleneck sweater. "I feel like a snowman," Al said. "And I'm nervous."

"You do not look like a snowman and don't be nervous. You will enjoy this more than I can say and I'll be with you every step of the way. Or rather, you'll be with me every step of the way."

"Thank goodness for that. So the parade begins at half past six."

Santa nodded. "And it is quite a parade. It lasts three hours. We'll watch most of it from the crystal bartizan."

Al pressed his hands to his stomach. "The butterflies!"

Santa chuckled. "Shall we meet in the foyer in half an hour? I always like to walk through the city and schmooze a bit before the parade begins. Chin wag, shake hands, pose for photographs. It means a lot to the elves."

"Of course!"

Santa started off, but then turned back. "Is anything the matter ... other than your butterflies?"

"I feel a bit muddled, I suppose," Al admitted. He came closer. "So we'll walk through the streets and visit and whatnot and we'll make our way to the castle to watch the parade. Then, toward the end of it, we will join the parade."

"That's right."

"And then we will do the inaugural ride."

"Yes. Over the city first and then … over the world."

"That's what I can't quite wrap my brain around," Al fretted.

"I remember feeling the same way, but there is nothing for you to do but ride along and enjoy. The real work has been done by flight logistics, engineers and mechanics. And it will be done by flight control and gift distribution and several other departments. This is our big night, but it's their big night, as well. We are never alone in this," Santa said, gripping Al's shoulder. "To be honest, it sometimes feels we're the mere figurehead. The blessed, fortunate figurehead. We represent Christmas. We represent love and giving. That is what tonight is about."

Al nodded and murmured his understanding.

"Alfred, dear man, I could tell you everything that will happen step by step but, even if I did, you won't fully grasp it until you've lived it. None of us can."

"It's as if I know it in my mind, but—"

"But there is nothing to compare it to," Santa finished for him. "Try not to worry. It will be the time of your life."

"Thank you."

Santa gave him a warm smile. "Don't forget to wear your new gloves."

"I won't. They're very nice."

"There is also a microchip in them you'll need," Santa said.

~~~

The crowd of elves gathered for the parade was bigger than ever and socializing with them was no less enjoyable than before. Santa had dreaded being without his wife, but he had Al by his side and that was special. Being in full dress uniform always added an element of pride and delight for everyone.

Al's jaw had dropped at the sight of the magnificently tailored red jacket of quality red wool. "I thought it was velvet," he'd remarked even as he eyed the sumptuous, white fur collar, cuffs and trim of Santa's suit. "Is that mink?"

"No. Ferox," Santa explained. "The ferox sheds its fur. There is no killing involved. They are farm raised. They also make wonderful pets."

Al's jacket, in contrast to Santa's, was white merino wool and fell to his knees. He wore a matching white kubanka hat, and looked quite dapper in it.

Most of the Manor elves were in the city for the festivities. Vestor took pride in introducing his brother Bonjovial who shared Vestor's fascination with human current events, especially pop music. Bon told them he'd written a Christmas ditty for humans and shyly asked if they would hear it. They were only too glad to hear it, they replied, so Bon pulled out a harmonica with a trembling hand and played a note. A small choir around him, including Vestor, hummed the note. After a big inhale, they began to sing.

"Let's put all worries behind us as friends remind us to not wait but celebrate the holiday. There's so much joy to share with loved ones everywhere, and Santa will soon be on his way." (The last line was sung by an adorable little elfkin.) *"I want some North Pole and mistletoe and greeting cards from friends we know. I can't wait to celebrate the holiday. There are so many gifts to share with loved ones everywhere. It won't be long until Christmas day. Let luh-uh-ov flow,*

let our hearts fill and grow. Let us lend a hand to our fellow man, so everyone can know-oh-oh ...a carol singing, bell ringing, snow flinging, laugher bringing, magical fantastical holiday. Stockings up, fill them up, sound the horn, pop some corn. Let's all celebrate the holiday!"

Santa, Al, and everyone around them applauded with gusto. "Wonderful," Santa cried.

"Thank you," Bon replied. He was all smiles. "Thank you so much," he said again when the excited clamor died down. "Um, Santa, I was wondering. Do you know Katy Perry?"

Santa cocked his head, confused by the name.

"Katheryn Hudson," Vestor interjected. "California, born in 84, I believe."

"Oh! Yes. Pentecostal parents."

"That's her," Vestor and Bon said in unison.

"I haven't seen Katy in years," Santa replied. "But she was always a good girl."

"Well," Bon said, "she's a singer, a very popular singer, and I hoped perhaps she could sing the song."

"I suppose we could get it to her," Santa said. "It would have to be anonymously. It is very catchy."

"Thank you, Santa!"

"I'll take care of getting it to transport," Vestor said, every bit as thrilled as Bon.

~~~

Santa and Al watched the parade in the crystal bartizan of the castle as they enjoyed a light meal. There were bands, acrobats, miniature fireworks, grand floats, drum corps, giant toys and strange, amazing contraptions. Elves lined the streets and cheered at everything that passed their way. Al occasionally stood and broke into applause, although no one could hear it.

When they finished dessert, Santa stood. "Shall we?" He started from the room with Al hot on his heels. "We'll take the chute and underpass to Station A where the flying team is waiting."

"You were right," Al said. "I am having the time of my life."

Santa laughed merrily. "Dear man, you haven't seen anything yet!"

"Hello," Santa called as he and Al approached the readied sleigh, the flying team, Julep and his under-trainers.

"Hello," they called back.

"The sleigh is magnificent," Al cried. "It is so much larger than I imagined."

The tall sleigh with intricate silver scrollwork and silver runners was polished to a high shine. There was a cushioned front seat of green velvet, and a cargo hold in back that held a large bag that seemed stuffed to capacity. The rear of the sleigh stood seven feet tall. The front of it stood five feet tall, the right height for driving while seated. The exterior's front was embossed with SC. Santa looked it all over as tears blurred his vision. He brushed his eyes with a gloved hand.

"Are you ready?" Julep asked tenderly.

Santa nodded and discreetly cleared his throat. "I am." He looked back at Al who was still marveling over the sleigh. "Are you ready?"

"I hope so," Al replied. "My worst fear is to let anyone down."

"You won't," the trainers exclaimed.

"You won't," Santa echoed calmly. He went to greet the reindeer as the trainers surrounded Al with words of encouragement.

Mostly.

"Are you prone to getting airsick? Or seasick?" DeGrue asked.

"No. Why?" Al asked worriedly.

Santa faced the lead reindeer and petted their necks. "Kasick, Fabian. Our last ride together, old friends." The reindeer grunted. Fabian looked away, fearful of becoming emotional. "It's all right, Fabian," Santa whispered to him before going to the next pair. The reindeer had red leather harnesses and colorful half blankets, more like a shawls, around their upper backs. Every year featured a new design and this year's was as exquisite as ever.

"Tylock, Azder," Santa said. "It's been a privilege." The reindeer stomped and grunted. "Thank you," Santa replied. "I feel the same." He moved back. "Maximus," he said fondly, patting the reindeer before turning to his partner. "Thelphius, follow Max's lead and you will not go wrong." Thelphius nodded first and then Maximum did the same. Santa moved to the last two reindeer in the lineup. "Deon, Gemini, don't be nervous. You'll be fine. I promise." They grunted and stomped. "That's the spirit!" Santa turned around. "All right," he said in a thick voice as he exited the row. "Let's go." He walked around and climbed up in the sleigh.

Al quickly followed him. He glanced at the controls on the dashboard. "It seems even taller when you're up here, doesn't it?"

"There are seat belts and straps to hang onto," Santa replied.

"I'll be fine. My balance has always been good."

"All right. Two things," Santa said. "Firstly, there's an earpiece in your pocket that you'll need for instructions from Control." He paused as Al found it and clipped it in place. "Secondly, so you know, the sleigh is on glide rails, so when it's time, it will rise and hover above the ground, making it easy for the reindeer to pull. You may sit or stand, but sitting is probably easier."

"I'll stand."

Santa grinned. "So be it." He took reins in hand. "Onward, my deer," he called.

The team pranced in unison with their antlers held high. The sleigh lifted suddenly enough that Al fell back into the seat laughing giddily. He quickly got back up and worked to steady himself. "Did I boast I had good balance?"

Santa chuckled. "Did you?"

"At least the seat is well padded," Al murmured.

"For good reason."

Joyous jazz music was playing as they reached the start of the parade route. Santa and Al waved and the elves cheered and waved back.

"Who knew they liked jazz?" Al said.

"They have marvelous jazz clubs here," Santa replied. As they reached the crowd, the elves began to sing *The Man With the Bag*. "Speaking of which," Santa said, "haul the bag up here, will you? All elfkins get a gift."

Al hauled the heavy bag up on the seat. "Are the gifts all the same?"

"Oh, no. They're chosen just as carefully as for human children."

"Then how will we know—"

"The microchip in our gloves. Just look at the elfkin, reach into the bag and the GI team, gift intelligence, monitors and matches the gift to the child. They've been observing where elves are lined up and rearranging gifts for the sake of ease."

"Ah!"

"They'll also feed you each name as you need it." Santa smiled at an elfkin in her mother's arms. "Bella," he greeted, reaching into the bag. "Here you are, dear. Merry Christmas."

The shy elfkin hugged her mother's neck, who accepted the gift with a smile and filled eyes. "Thank you, Santa."

"Geeves," Al said. He reached into the bag and handed the gift that came to him to a young male elf. "Happy Christmas."

"Thank you!"

Young elves were hastening forward, older siblings leading younger ones in a happy, expectant rush.

"Nalarys," Santa greeted. "Hello, dear!"

"Stephano Tasselton," Al called. "Merry Christmas." Gifts were handed out left and right. "I've never been a star before," Al said to Santa during a momentary break.

"Co-star," Santa teased and they both laughed. The parade had always been a pleasure, but Al's unmitigated joy added an element of delight.

At the end of the route, they continued driving. They reached the city limits and the reindeer broke into a run that forced Al back into the seat again. They slowed and turned around in a field and Al stood watching the trainers and several of the hands hurrying toward them with large clear objects, like giant butterfly wings. He watched in rapt fascination as sets of wings were fitted to each pair of reindeer. "I feel like I should understand what's going on," he said, "but I don't."

"We're about to take our inaugural ride over the city."

"And those contraptions they are strapping to the reindeer?"

"Wings, of course. Reindeer can't fly without them. That and the lift from the glide rails and the propeller that is on back of the sleigh."

Al swallowed. "Perhaps I will sit." He sat and fumbled to fasten his seatbelt and find the strap on the side of the sleigh.

One of the reindeer hands hurried over to him with a blanket. "Here you are," he said. "Have a good ride!"

"Ooh, it's warmed," Al said with appreciation as he took it. "Thank you, Machel."

"Ready," Julep called. "Up on eight!"

Machel hurriedly backed away from the sleigh.

"Here we go," Santa cried. He whirled a whip around and cracked it in the air and the reindeer dashed forward for *one, two, three, four,* going at a full run now, *five, six, seven, eight* – and they leapt as the strength of the air flow from the glide rail increased, more in front than in back, and the propeller engaged. *Uuuuup* they went. It never failed to thrill Santa, not even on this fifty-ninth time.

They rode over the city, waving down at the wildly cheering elves. Santa banked westward and they sailed over villages and farms where elves were no less joyous. Al unbuckled his seatbelt and stood clutching the side rail with one hand and hugging the blanket with the other.

"It's fantastic," Al called.

It really was. They circled around to pass ranches, more villages, forestland and a river. They dipped over Fenland Forest where every reindeer watched and every elf waved with pride and excitement.

Santa's Manor was glorious from above. The annexes behind it glowed. Elves were on the roof of Annex A watching and jumping for joy. Santa spotted the exit ramp, made from snow and compressed air, and geared the engine down. The wings on the lead pair of reindeer began to retract while those in the back stayed open. Santa cut the engine. "Have to go nearly weightless here for a moment," he called. He pressed a button, his stomach lurched, and it felt as if they were floating although they were still going down team first. There was a jolt when reindeer hooves connected with the ramp. "Now to break," Santa said. They reached the bottom of the ramp and went another thirty yards before stopping. They were close to Annex B.

Al collapsed on the seat again. "I think I may have left my stomach up there!"

"Wonderful job," Santa called to the reindeer.

Reindeer hands and trainers and elves were rushing to them. Santa could not stop smiling as he sat next to Al. "Before next year, you'll practice in the simulator until you're comfortable."

"That's good to know."

The elves reached them and began unharnessing the reindeer amidst cheers and compliments.

"Thank you," Santa called. "It was as wonderful as ever." He rose and climbed down with a bit of assistance. He turned to Al as he climbed down on wobbly looking legs. "Now we prepare for the big ride," Santa said.

Chapter Fifteen
Fabulous Earth

Al followed Santa into Annex B, a place he had hardly seen, and stopped short to see a strange looking spacecraft. The main body was a glass orb that contained two seats. In the front of the cabin was a long, almost clear area that ended in a point. Behind and below the cabin were engines.

"This isn't like the vessel that transported me here," Al said with a shake of his head.

"You're right," Santa replied. "That was what they call the bullet. Very straightforward. Strap you in, get you here. Not much a view and shrouded from human surveillance."

"And this?"

"This is the Christmas Ship, of course. It is meant to be seen, at least, some of the time." He noticed Marencourt striding toward them. "If you want to attend to any personal needs," Santa said to Al, "You should do it now."

"Everything is in order," Marencourt reported when he reached them. "The route is locked in and all teams are standing by."

"Good," Santa said. "Excuse me while I hit the little elves room." He started off.

"So this is what we ride tonight," Al said in bemusement. "But where are the gifts?"

"Have a glass of water," Santa called. "Have a tinkle. We'll be on our way soon."

An elf cheered to hear it. Another burst into song, "*Santa Claus is coming to town.*"

"But—" Al sputtered.

"Worry not," Marencourt said before he walked away.

~~~

"All right," Santa said when they had been securely strapped in. All around them was a bustle of activity. Elves were looking over equipment, checking handheld devices, comparing notes and evaluating.

"Everything seems smooth?" Al sputtered. "This is all normal?"

"Perfectly normal. Take some nice, deep breaths and I'll explain what's about to happen."

Al nodded and took a breath.

"After we launch," Santa said, "we do periphery circuits of earth. We will be too high for anyone to make us out, but that's where most of the gifting occurs."

"Where are the gifts?"

"We don't handle them. There isn't room. The GI team transports them to the homes directly beneath us. There are more than five thousand highly trained elves on the task. For us, the first part of the journey feels like massively rapid movement, too fast to make sense of. It's the next parts that are more fun."

"The next parts," Al repeated. "Which are?"

"First, going close to earth so we can be seen. Keep the legend alive. It's also where our sight-seeing happens. Every year, flight logistics will give you a choice of locations. Do you want to fly over the Eiffel

Tower? The Great Wall? Angel Falls of Venezuela? Ask and they'll set it up. Cities are the best to see because it's midnight as we pass over."

Al exhaled as he imagined it. "What are the other fun parts?"

"Personal deliveries. Every Santa does them at some point in his tenure. I haven't done many in a few years and I don't plan to tonight."

"Personal deliveries?"

Santa nodded. "Going into homes to leave the gifts."

"Of course. Yes."

"We're good here," an elf called giving a thumbs up.

"I should tell you a funny story," Santa said.

Elves were backing away. The engines were revving. "Now?" Al asked.

"Eh, why not? So, many years ago, I was transported down to deliver gifts to a home. I didn't know which home or even what country I was in. It was one of my first home-excursions. All I knew is that I was sitting right here and then I felt tingly and light as air and then I reformulated in a home. A nice home. Gold shag carpet, metallic orange and gold wallpaper. But don't judge, it was the seventies."

"I remember the seventies," Al replied absentmindedly as he watched the elves. His hands were so tightly clenched, his knuckles were white.

"I put the gifts under the tree and made my way to the table to sample cookies they'd left. Snickerdoodles. *Mmm*."

"Is there anything we should be doing?" Al asked nervously.

"No. We're merely passengers at his point. Anyway, I turned, ready to go, and got the shock of my life to see a man staring at me from several yards away. A large, black man in a Santa suit. I was flabbergasted! We're not supposed to be transported into any home with adults who are awake and yet, there he stands, as shocked as I am. I instantly knew he must have just come from a holiday party or else he had dressed as Santa in case he was spotted by his children putting out gifts. Something like that. Well, I drew a breath to explain who I was, and he did the same thing. Of course, neither of us said a word. I took a step forward with my hand outstretched and he did the same. That's when I realized I was looking in a mirror."

"A mirror?"

"Yes. A large mirror in their entry hall. Still, something did not add up. I glanced around and saw the cutest child, he must have been four or five, peeking around the corner."

The Christmas Ship began to move and Al stiffened. The vehicle shifted until the nose was facing straight up. The ceiling had opened so Santa and Al were on their backs staring up at a vast starry sky.

"Richard was his name," Santa said.

"Whose name?" Al asked breathlessly.

Santa glanced at him. "The boy, of course. You see, my appearance had changed to be what he expected Santa to look like. So I gave him a wink and a smile and—" Santa placed his finger aside his nose, "Got out of there."

"Reindeer check," said a voice through their headsets.

Suddenly, in front of the capsule was a hologram of a team of reindeer. At the head of them was one with a red nose.

"Rudolph," Al exclaimed.

"Give the children what they want," Santa replied with a chuckle.

"Let's have them run," an elf said over the intercom.

The reindeer in the projection began a simulated run.

"Good to go," another voice said.

The hologram vanished.

"Sleigh illusion," an elf called.

The sides of the glass orb suddenly looked like a sleigh. Then the illusion disappeared.

"All systems are go!"

"Remember to breathe," Santa said.

"Ten, nine, eight," began the countdown.

"You okay?" asked Santa.

Al gulped a breath.

"… three, two, one—"

There was a roar of the engines, the capsule vibrated, and they were propelled into the night sky. They were moving too fast to make out anything. There were just lights and movement, movement and light. Dots and zig-zags of lights. Santa's chest felt heavy, but it always did. He closed his eyes appreciating the magnificence of what they were doing. *Happy Christmas, world!*

It wasn't until the next phase of the trip that they were able to speak again. As the craft lowered through the stratosphere and their speed dropped, Santa looked at Al and asked how he was doing.

"I don't know," Al stammered. "Fine, I think?"

"You are more than fine. Welcome to the troposphere." He hit a button and the reindeer and sleigh projections appeared. It looked as if Santa's sleigh was being pulled by nine reindeer.

Al glanced behind them and gasped to see the engine had vanished. "Santa!"

"Don't worry. The engines are cloaked, but they're still working." Santa looked at the each of the instruments on the panel. "Everything looks good."

Below them was shining, moonlit ocean. "Look at that over there," Al marveled. "It's glowing blue."

"Phytoplankton. Just look how alive it is. How soothing, but also exotic. Don't you think? And speaking of exotic, look."

Al peered at the colorful, glamorous cityscape ahead. So bright and varied and busy. "Beautiful."

"Taiwan," Santa said. "That's the rainbow bridge."

Santa adjusted a control and the ship lifted before covering more ocean. They lowered again, nearly skimming the surface of the water. Al squealed. Santa laughed. "Dolphins," Al called as a line of them jumped.

"And here we have Australia," Santa said.

Al gaped as they passed the Harbour Bridge and the Opera House." "Oh, my," he breathed.

Close to New Zealand, Santa engaged the auto pilot. It was the best way to experience the glaciers, mountains, beaches and mysterious wonders of the island country. Al seemed to be melting back into his seat and Santa knew the feeling. Time seemed to stand still as they passed over Argentina, Paraguay, Peru and Venezuela. What a big and incredible world it was. It was almost too much to take in.

They soared above Mexico and into the United States traveling from Texas into the Midwest, past Wisconsin and into Ontario. "It will be soon, now," Santa said lethargically. Realm travel took it out of him after a few million miles. There was a rush of altitude, the reindeer disappeared, and the engines engaged to full power.

Back in Elfrealm, the Christmas Ship backed into Annex B. It docked and the front of the capsule lowered until the passengers were facing front. The glass of the orb lifted from the front, opening the cabin, and retracted into the rear of the vehicle. There was elf activity all around them, but Santa and Al remained motionless.

"I don't know that I can move," Al said.

"You can't. Not without help."

"Is this what a jellyfish feels like?" Al asked.

"I don't know," Santa replied. "I've never asked one."

Al was assisted out first and helped into a chair on glide-rails by two HHE's.

"See you about lunch time," Santa called.

"All right," Al replied. "What time is it?" Al asked his helpers.

"It's the wee hours of Christmas morning," one replied.

Santa looked over to find Marencourt standing there with a pleased grin on his face.

"Everything seems to have gone well," Marencourt commented. "How do you feel?"

"Like a jellyfish."

Marencourt looked bemused as he waved attendants in. They helped Santa out of the ship and into a chair.

"Nighty, night," Marencourt called as Santa was pushed onward.

Santa was beyond fatigued. The exhaustion had never been quite so dramatic before. Back in his room, two elves, Ollie and Huntress Fettleput, removed his boots and struggled to undress him. Bless their hearts; he did not have the strength to help. They got off his jacket and trousers and decided that was good enough. He flopped back into bed on top of his covers and they could not quite manage to get him up again.

"Let's just throw a cover over him," Ollie suggested.

"No," Huntross retorted. "He must go under the sheets properly."

They called in more help, Tindie and Angelo, which did not solve the problem. He was too heavy for the four of them and he was too drained to be of any assistance as much as he would have preferred it.

Exxem, sometimes referred to as Exxem know-it-all behind his back, entered. "The solution is so obvious," he scoffed. "You two get on that side of him," he bossed. Ollie, Tindie, this side. Extend two fingers and slide them just underneath him."

"Of course," Ollie said.

"Light as a feather, stiff as a board," they all chanted. Santa's body began to lift. "Light as a feather, stiff as a board." Higher he went until he was a foot off the bed, the maximum their outstretched arms would allow.

Exxem scrambled underneath him and began to pull back the covers and sheet. "How the lot of you would ever manage without me, I don't know," he grumbled.

The four lifters exchanged disgusted looks and withdrew their fingers. Down went Santa right on top of Exxem.

"Get. Him. Off," Exxem wheezed.

"Come now," Santa managed to scold, albeit halfheartedly. Exxem really did bring things upon himself. The chant began again, his body was lifted, the bed covers were withdrawn, and he was set down and covered.

"I'll get even with you," Exxem swore to the others. "Goodnight, Santa."

"Do you need anything?" Huntross asked Santa.

"No, thank you," Santa replied weakly.

"Goodnight, Santa," they said before trooping out. And the lights went out.

<u>Chapter Sixteen</u>
Christmas

"Oh, dear," Santa said when he looked in the mirror late the next morning. Last night's trek had taken it out of him. He had slept in, had breakfast in bed and enjoyed a long shower using all six nozzles to the optimum directions and strengths. Of course, this was the time of the term when aging accelerated.

He dressed in a favorite fuzzy greenish-blue sweater that somehow seemed too big all of a sudden, sweat pants which seemed a loose, happy socks and house shoes. He started toward his door noticing a sturdy walking cane that had mysteriously appeared. Admittedly, using it eased the pressure on his right knee, so he took hold of it. Why should he be stubborn about using it?

He left his room and saw a smiling, youthful Al walking toward him. The age transformation had taken place. Santa had thought he was prepared for it, but Al's alteration was so dramatic, he was shocked. He was a handsome fellow.

"I don't think we've met, sir," Al teased. He stuck his hand out. "Al Dorsett at your service."

"Kris Kringle," Santa said as they shook. "No, I don't believe we have met. Although I may have met your father. Old gent running around the place with more vigor than any chap his age should have?"

Al laughed. "Happy Christmas, Santa."

"Happy Christmas to you. I would ask how you're feeling, but it's obvious. It's not quite fair, really. I aged ten years last night and you woke up twenty-five years younger."

"More like twenty-seven, but who's counting?"

"Indeed."

"That was quite a journey we had," Al said with a shake of his head. "It defies description. It almost didn't seem real this morning, but I went to the viewing room and witnessed it and hundreds of children delighted with our gifts."

Santa nodded. "I'm going there now."

"I am going down to wait for CJ. She might arrive any time. Do you want to come?"

"You go ahead. Why don't we all meet for an early dinner? Say six o'clockish?"

"That sounds good. I can't wait for you to meet her." Al hurried on with a skip in his step.

Santa went to the viewing room at a far slower pace. There was much to see this morning. Human recordings of the sleigh in motion, people catching a glimpse of it, caught up in the wonder of the moment. There was also a replay of the places they had seen. Of even greater interest, were the children. He sat and got comfortable. "May I begin with a highlight of the Follett family, please?"

On Christmas Eve night, Sam stood back watching critically as Frank stuck the last artificial limb in the pole completing the five-foot Christmas tree that had to be fifty years old. "There," he said. He looked at Sam and she looked at him. "I'll admit it's seen better days," he said. He looked at it again. "It'll look better with lights on it." He went to the box with lights and pulled up a tangled web.

"Mom got new ones today," Sam said.

He looked at her. "Did she? Good. I'm not even sure these are safe. I haven't had the thing up in years."

Judging by the scent and the sound of it, Beth was cooking in the kitchen while singing with the radio. Sierra was asleep on the couch.

"I'll go get them," Sam said hurrying to the kitchen.

Frank eyed the tree critically. When Sam walked back in with a bag, he said, "Next year, we'll get a real tree."

Sam looked up at him with a strange expression. Wary, almost afraid to hope. She handed him the bag and he pulled out a box of lights and began opening it.

"Can I pick it out?" Sam asked.

"The tree? Yes. You and Sierra. I don't see why not. As long as your mother likes it."

Sam sat cross-legged on the floor and started looking through an old box of ornaments. "Do you think we'll still be here next year?" she asked without looking up.

"Unless you've planned a trip around the world I don't know about."

She giggled.

"Have you?" he asked worriedly.

She shook her head.

"Well, then, yes. I think you will be here next Christmas and the one after that and the one after that. But if you do plan a trip around the world, can I go, too?"

She nodded.

"Good. That's settled then."

Sam hugged her knees. "Papaw Frank?"

"*Hmm?*"

"Do you think Santa knows we're here?"

"I know he does." He walked over and plugged the colorful strand in and then sat on a stool and began winding them through the bottom branches.

"How do you know?"

"I just do."

"How?"

He stopped what he was doing and looked at her. "I'm old, so I know lots of things."

She made a face at the unsatisfactory answer.

"For example, I know that you wrote Santa and asked him for a home."

She gasped in surprise that he knew this.

"And, once you did that, Santa had his elves contact me because he knew that we would make a good family. I agreed and asked your mother if she wanted the arrangement, she said yes and here we all are. So, yes, Santa knows you're here."

She didn't say anything for a moment. "Is that for real?"

He nodded and made a crisscross on his heart.

Beth bustled back into the room. "Oh, sleepy girl," she said when she saw her youngest sleeping. Beth folded her arms and tried not to smirk at the pathetic looking tree. "I think it will look wonderful when it's all done."

"We're going to get a real one next year," Sam announced. "And I get to pick it out."

Frank chuckled as he went back to stringing the lights.

"Excellent," Santa murmured. "Now let's see Liam and Tommy."

"Tommy," Liam whispered urgently in the dark.

After a moment, Santa could make out Tommy's sleeping form and his younger brother trying to shake him awake.

"Tommy!"

"Dude," Tommy complained. "What? I'm sleeping."

"The alarm went off."

"What?"

"The bells. The alarm. The strings got pulled. Santa!"

Tommy groaned. "Go back to sleep."

"No. He was here."

"Great. Then we'll have presents in the morning."

"There's presents now! Not the ones Dad set out, either. These ones have gold wrapping."

Tommy rolled over to face him. "What do you mean the ones Dad set out?" he asked sheepishly.

Liam rolled his eyes. "He always does after he thinks I'm asleep. And he takes a bite out of the cookies." He huffed. "Like Santa would really eat them after that."

Tommy sighed. "Can we just check it out in the morning?"

Liam shook his head.

Tommy sat and swung his legs around. "Okay. Let's get it over with."

They walked out into the living room where Tommy stopped short to see gold-wrapped boxes that had not been there before. He walked closer to an

133

envelope hanging on the tree. It was addressed to him in old-world lettering.

"Open it," Liam urged.

Tommy pulled it off and took out a piece of elegant parchment with more fancy writing.

"What's it say? Who's it from?"

Tommy didn't answer as he finished reading. He looked down at Liam. "Did you write Santa and take back your wish for the car?"

Liam nodded.

"So that I would do well on my SAT's?"

Liam hesitated and then nodded again.

"Oh, man." Tommy dropped down and wrapped Liam in his arms. "You are best brother in the world."

"You are," Liam said.

Their dad walked in still half asleep. "What's going on? It's twelve thir—" He broke off mid word to see the gifts. "What is this? Was Catherine here? Did she do this?"

The boys shook their heads. "Santa," Liam said.

Curt looked at Tommy, who nodded. "I guess it was our turn." He smiled at his brother. "Thanks to somebody I know."

"What is—" Curt began.

Tommy rose and handed him the letter. Curt took it and read. He got an incredulous expression on his face and looked at Tommy who nodded meaningfully. "I've been given the best prep course out there. The thing costs like twelve hundred bucks."

Curt was too stunned to reply. He looked around at the gifts. "What the heck?"

"Can I open one, Dad?" Liam asked.

Curt was having difficulty speaking. "Sure. I guess."

Liam pulled out a box with his name on it and tore into it. It was a deluxe remote-control car. "I got it anyway," he cried happily.

"He's going to have three of them," Curt said quietly.

"Yeah," Tommy gaped. "But that's one of the good ones." He was already moving closer.

Curt scratched his head, befuddled.

"One more, Daddy?" Liam pleaded.

Curt plodded forward and sat on the floor between his sons. "Yeah, okay. I mean, it is Christmas."

Santa was so proud of his think tank. They had done good work. But then his smile dimmed. "And now Lakeisha."

Lakeisha was sitting on her bed working a crossword puzzle in a book. It was Christmas morning and she was alone in the room she shared with another girl. There were sounds of talking, laughter and music from nearby. On the foot of her bed were unwrapped gifts, socks and a dream-catcher craft kit.

A six year-old girl named Olivia came into their room still wearing her pajamas and carrying a doll. "Look what I got," she said. She sat on Lakeisha's bed and passed over her doll. "The box said her name was Dana but I named her Keisha."

Lakeisha smiled. "She's cool."

"She has glasses, too, but I let Hannah play with them. She got a doll, too. Hers has red hair."

Lakeisha passed the doll back. "Keisha, huh?"

The little girl nodded.

"Hey," Darcy said cheerfully as she came in. "Thanks for the present."

Lakeisha shrugged. "Not like I bought it. But you're welcome."

Darcy came closer to show the necklace she was wearing. "I love it."

"It looks good."

Emma popped her head in. "There's doughnuts," she called. "C'mon."

Lakeisha set the crossword book aside. It had been her 'secret Santa' gift from one of the other kids. "I'm in," she said as she swung her legs around the far side of the bed, bumping a box on the floor she hadn't realized was there. It had gold wrapping with frilly ribbons and it had a tag with her name on it. She picked it up, blinking in surprise. It was at least twice as big as a shoe box and heavier.

"What is that?" Darcy exclaimed.

Emma came closer to see and Olivia got on all fours on the bed.

"I have no idea," Lakeisha replied. She hesitated tearing into it because she had never seen a prettier gift.

"Open it," Emma urged.

Lakeisha took off the wrapping paper as carefully as she could in case she could reuse it sometime. Inside was a box with a very real looking toy cat.

A cat! Her letter to Santa! But she had sealed the envelope, addressed it and put it in the mailbox herself. She hadn't told anybody, so who could have known? She pulled the cat from the box and it meowed.

"Oh my gosh," Emma cried. She dashed to the door and hollered, "Come see what Keisha got!"

Lakeisha pulled the cat close and it purred. And moved.

"That is so freaking cool," Darcy said as she touched it. "It's soft. It's just like a real cat."

"Can I see?" Olivia asked.

Lakeisha felt weird as she passed it over for her to see. The cat meowed again and Olivia burst into laughter. "It meowed at me!"

"That is seriously like the coolest thing I've ever seen," Darcy said. "Who's it from?"

Keisha looked at the box and saw a note inside. She pulled it out. The signature was the first thing that jumped out at her. *Santa.*

Olivia leaned in and hugged her arm. "It's from Santa!"

Darcy was now holding the cat. She put in on the bed and it turned on its back and was moving its paws to her delight. Other kids were rushing in to see what the excitement was about. Lakeisha sat. She was remembering the day Miss Applegate had made them write to Santa. "Faith, you," her teacher had urged with a gleam in her eye. Lakeisha turned from the others and began reading the note.

Dear Lakeisha,
This cat will have to do until you have your own place. One day, you will have all the choices in the world, my girl. Until then, study hard, be a good friend and know how much I believe in you.
Best Regards,
Santa

Lakeisha's throat ached fiercely. Tears filled her eyes, so she couldn't turn around. The others would see. Not that anyone was noticing her. They were all captivated by the cat, each of them wanting a turn to hold it. She discreetly sniffed and wiped her face and then turned back around.

"It's so cool!"

"I want one!"

"Did you see that?"

"I wonder how much they cost?"

"What are you going to name it?"

"Not *it*! It's a girl. It's got a pink collar."

Darcy looked at her. "What *are* you going to name her?"

"Faith," Lakeisha said, deciding as she said it.

Darcy nodded and smiled. She seemed to get how close to tears Lakeisha was.

Lakeisha held her hands out. "Can I have her?" The cat was passed back to her and the kids started leaving. After all, there were doughnuts.

"I'll save you a doughnut, Keish," someone called.

"Can I play with Faith later?" someone else called.

Lakeisha hugged the cat and looked back down at the note, especially the line about Santa believing in her. Wow. Just wow.

Santa was touched and vastly relieved. "Merry Christmas, dear girl," he murmured.

~~~

Dinner that evening was enjoyable. CJ was lovely and delightful. She was also transport-lagged, and Santa knew the feeling. As he settled in to sleep that night, he reflected on how good it was to see Al so happy. All in all, this final Christmas had been a outstanding day.

<u>Chapter Seventeen</u>
The Sendoff

One foot in front of the other. Santa's arm was wobbly as he leaned on his cane, but he was walking on his own two feet. He only had to get past the goodbyes and make it to the vessel in Annex B. Marencourt was by his side and would never allow him to stumble or fall.

The upper corridor was packed with well-wishers. Santa smiled to see them all. The setting sun cast a pastel hue from the windows. He chuckled to see a group of twenty-seven elves wearing shirts with *STT* emblazoned on the front. They turned to show *Santa 2020* on the back. "I'm so proud of the work you did," Santa said to them with the little that was left of his voice.

"And will do," Marencourt added.

"Yes."

Al came forward to greet him. CJ was a step behind and already crying. Santa cupped her cheek and she nodded, unable to speak. "Enjoy yourself," he said softly. "And support this fellow here."

"I will," she managed.

"It has been such an honor," Al said shakily.

"The honor has been mine," Santa returned. "I leave Christmas in good hands."

The men embraced and then Al stepped back and bowed. CJ did as well. Santa moved on toward the pillar, but stopped as Vestor, who was crying as if his heart was broken, approached with Cassarina.

"Vestor," Santa said. "You've been invaluable, my friend. Thank you."

"We love you, Santa," Vestor blurted.

"And I love you." He looked at Ree and nodded. "Dear Ree."

Ree was barely holding back her emotion from overwhelming her. Elves were bowing to him. Some waved. Some were crying, others looked happy for him. Marencourt opened the casing on the pillar and the tube awaited. Santa glanced over the crowd again, nodded to Al, and stepped inside the tube. Marencourt followed.

"Annex B," Marencourt said before the door shut. When they were on their way, Marencourt spoke in a suspiciously tight voice. "Do not think for a moment that I'm going to break down and blubber."

"I don't," Santa replied. "But I do want to thank you."

Marencourt turned his face away.

"I fear I would have failed without you. Thank you, Marencourt. From the bottom of my heart."

Marencourt exhaled and reached up with both hands to wipe his face. Then he took a deep breath and faced front again. "I will miss our chess games."

Santa grinned. "I'll especially miss the ones I won."

"Four," Marencourt snapped. "Out of six hundred and fourteen games. Four!"

"Ah, but they were a remarkable four."

Marencourt snorted with laugher. The conveyance stopped, the door opened and Marencourt emerged first, his emotions once again under control. Only a tell-tale tear caught on his eyelash gave him away.

There was no crowd in Annex B as Santa was helped into the vessel. The crew was protective, silent and somber. Santa did not want to cry so he stared straight ahead. When the bubble closed around him and the craft started to move into position, he looked over and gave a final wave to Marencourt. The elf waved back, dangerously close to tears again.

In seconds, Santa was on his back, staring up at the darkening sky. The sun had set. A silvery-white projection shot out in front of him. He knew that once he was on his way, four more similar projections would shine from the center orb, forming a star. He remembered watching his predecessors' ascent to TGB. It had been breathtaking, those few unforgettable moments of significance and wonder.

This time the crew's countdown was silent. Santa knew blastoff was imminent from the tremor of the ship and sound of the engines. "See you soon, my love," he said with a wistful expression.

~~~

Al, CJ, and hundreds of elves had gathered outside the manor to watch Santa's departure. They were expecting it and yet it seemed unexpectedly sudden when the ship blasted off emblazoning a star with a long glittering tail across the sky. It exploded in glittering light momentarily revealing another realm. Sera was there, smiling and holding her arms out. In an instant, the sky was normal again, as if nothing had occurred. Oh, but it had occurred and it was spectacular.

Bells began tolling and fireworks shot up from the city in celebration of the past Santa and Mrs. Claus and the new. Al turned to CJ. She was trembling. They both were. "I will miss him," he admitted.

She nodded. "I wish I had gotten more time with him."

"I know. But it looks like it's our show now. Are you ready, Mrs. Claus?"

She leaned in and kissed him tenderly. "We will do our best, Mr. Claus. Will we not?"

"Yes, we will."

They turned back to watch the fireworks with their arms wrapped around one another.

Jane Shoup (Super) is an award-winning author of several novels and a children's picture book, *One Little Leaf.* She lives in Greensboro, North Carolina with her husband, Scott, and dog, Gabby, and near her three adult daughters and their families including four grandchildren.

Music has been a lifelong passion. If she's breathing, and not writing, she is frequently humming or singing, sometimes much to her family's chagrin. *Celebrate the Holiday* is her original composition. Visit her website at janeshoup.com for a link to hear the song.